Rescue Me

Sandy Nadeau

Rescue Me

Contact Information: titleadmin@pelicanbookgroup.com

Cover Art by *Nicola Martinez*

Harbourlight Books, a division of Pelican Ventures, LLC
www.pelicanbookgroup.com PO Box 1738 *Aztec, NM * 87410

Harbourlight Books sail and mast logo is a trademark of Pelican Ventures, LLC

Publishing History
First Harbourlight Edition, 2016
Electronic Edition ISBN 978-1-61116-496-1
Paperback Edition ISBN 978-1-61116-534-0
Published in the United States of America

Dedication

"Greater love has no one but this, that he lay down his life for his friends." John 15:13

Friends are one of the greatest gifts from God. Jesus, you are my "bestest" friend of all time! I'm married to my next best friend. Thirty-nine years so far. And having my daughter Trish be my best friend, too, priceless.
To Marcia, the world may have lost you this past year, but your unconditional friendship and love will be with me forever. Thank you for showing me what loving Jesus really means. Elaine, thanks for going along with me on this writing ride. To other friends I've watched pass from this life, thank you for being a part of my life. Karol, Gayle, and Penny, I hope you know what you meant to me. And to new friends and readers, I love getting to know you more. Thanks for coming along on this latest adventure.

What People are Saying

Romance is often complicated by life and Sandy Nadeau's RESCUE ME takes the reader through the obstacles that surround two people who have been wounded by those complications. Sandy pens a beautiful story of love overcoming all obstacles and God's perfect love healing all wounds. It's my pleasure to recommend RESCUE ME.

~Tracie Peterson, best-selling author of over one hundred novels including the Brides of Seattle *and* Lone Star Brides *series*

Other Titles by Sandy Nadeau

RED GOLD

1

"I can't believe this." Steve McNeal reached down again to try to move the rock that trapped his foot. Pain shot through his entire leg and cold dots of perspiration chilled his forehead. He rested against the granite boulder trying to ignore his throbbing ankle and to slow his heartbeat. Of course this had to happen. How could he have been so stupid as to try to scramble between the boulders alone? How many times had he scaled this boulder field? A shortcut to the trail. Brilliant idea.

Bracing both arms against the cold, rough granite on either side of him, he pushed with his free leg against a flatter area of one boulder, trying to get some relief from the pressure on his trapped foot. No doubt about it. This was a definite problem.

Steve scanned the sloping hillside that held the trail, which wound around the boulders that now held him hostage. The view was limited from his position, but at least he'd made his way down facing forward so he could look out instead of at the rock behind him.

Unbelievable. Ten feet from the ground, the trail right there, freedom so close and yet absolutely unattainable. *Ow!* He had to get his foot out. Or quit moving.

How could there be no one on the trail today? He twisted his upper body to look up at the boulders. "Anybody up there?" He quickly straightened. *Ouch, OK that hurts.* He reached into his pocket and pulled out his cellphone for the tenth time. Still no bars. What did he expect? Suddenly he'd have signal?

Cell towers were not a popular thing among the dwellers of the foothills southwest of Denver.

"Lord, a little help here?"

"Hey, Mister."

It might as well have been a voice from heaven. Relief let some of the tension out of his shoulders. He strained to see the face that peered over the edge of the rocks above.

"What'cha doin' down there?"

"Hey kid, I'm uh…stuck. Can you go get some help?" Steve's arm slid against the granite and a little skin peeled off as he tried to look up at the boy. More pain burned a path through his leg, and he gritted his teeth to keep from moaning. His forehead tightly furrowed. He didn't want to look like a sissy in front of the kid.

"Who are you talking to?" A female voice asked.

"There's a guy down there."

"Oh, my. Are you OK?"

Seriously? Do I look OK? "No ma'am. I appear to be trapped by a rock. Can you get a call out for help?" Steve couldn't see much of her between his position and only her eyes peeking over the edge.

"I don't have a signal. We'll go where we can get one. Hang in there."

Not much choice. "Thanks."

The footsteps moved away. Back to the quiet of the woods. Steve tried to remember where the cell signals could be received in the park. He never really paid attention while out here. Making a call was the last thing he wanted to do while hiking. He hoped they wouldn't have to go all the way to the parking lot. They'd have to wait for the crew, and then get back up here. That would add at least thirty or forty more minutes to his confinement than he cared to think about.

He dreaded which of his colleagues would be on duty today with rescue, not to mention the fire department. Was Ronnie on today? As the climbing expert on the department, it was likely she'd respond. He liked seeing her anytime, but not under these circumstances, given the choice. This ranked right up there as his most humiliating moment. Well, maybe not, but at the moment it felt that way. The fact that she wouldn't want to see him didn't help.

Breath expelled out of him, inflating his left cheek. Repositioning his upper body to find any level of comfort, he closed his eyes to see the image of her in his mind. He missed Ronnie since she broke it off a few years ago, but this would not be the way to encourage her back into a relationship.

He knew the drill. He was a firefighter, for crying out loud. He had given the talk to countless grade-schoolers. Never hike alone. Stick with a buddy. Sheesh. How humiliating. He'd never live this down.

The heavy scent of fresh pine and forest debris filled his nostrils. A chipmunk skittered down below, free as could be.

"Show off." Irritation rose up inside and increased as he took it out on the wildlife. "You're losing it, Steve." He roared against the pain developing in his stuck lower leg, reminding him of the guy who had to cut his own arm off. He, too, had been out alone, and after days of a rock trapping his arm, with no help in sight, the man had no choice but to amputate his own arm to make it out alive.

The pain started to bring on desperate thoughts of how to escape this mess he'd gotten himself into. "Maybe..." He looked down at his leg. No, Ronnie would still know what a stupid thing he did. Even more stupid if he cut his own leg off. They'd get him some help, right? He hoped they realized this was serious.

With little else to do, the thought wouldn't leave him. Amputation would make his job as a firefighter a bit difficult. He resigned himself to wait. Wait for her to come to his rescue. He groaned. Maybe she would have today off. Ah, one could hope.

Again he pulled his leg and tried to reposition or better yet, wrench it free, but it put his ankle that much closer to breaking. He had to refocus and began to analyze the position of his foot. He had his forearms wedged against the rough granite in a desperate attempt to try to keep his weight from causing further damage to the tendons in his foot. It continued to scrape his arms raw.

Someone—a skinny someone—would have to raise the rock from below to free his foot. A skinny person could fit in the gap beneath him between the two boulders, and he knew who that would end up being. He couldn't see any other way, outside of an earthquake shaking it loose.

Voices echoed up to him from the path through the forest. *How am I ever going to live this down?* He moaned as his head fell backward, seeing only sky.

The team came up the trail toward the rocks. Finally. Pine needles crunching, gravel sliding as they rushed to reach his self-inflicted prison. The young eyes he'd seen looking over the top of the rocks and the woman who resembled the boy pointed toward him. As all the faces looked up, he saw her.

Ronnie.

He knew it. She would have to be on when something like this happened. And Troy, the obnoxious rookie on the fire department. Great. Of course, they both had to be on call.

In an attempt to keep his humor about

him, he raised his hand in a half-hearted wave. "Nice of you all to join me."

Ronnie's forehead scrunched, her eyes filled with…was that concern? "Steve. What in the world…?" She dropped her gear and came near the base of the rocks to evaluate his situation.

"I know, I know. I'm stuck, OK? Just get me out of here."

"You bonehead," Troy piped in. "What were you thinking?"

The team of rescue and fire department personnel followed her up the slope as close to the rock face as they could and set their gear down. The team leader, George, walked over to the narrow opening under Steve and examined the situation.

"Looks like we can dislodge the rock from below you, Steve." George explained the plan to the crew then directed two men to take the harness and ropes up top. He pointed to the route a little ways to his left. "Well, Ronnie, you're the thinnest, you need to get in there and try to push up on the rock to release it. Steve, do you think it's broken?"

"No, I don't think so. It won't budge."

Troy took Ronnie's arm to lead her up to the gap.

Ronnie gave him a scowl and pulled her arm away then worked her way into the area on her own. She tightened the chin strap of her climbing helmet as she worked her way into the cavity and climbed on some of the long, fallen rocks, testing their stability. She looked up and smiled.

Did she have to be so cute?

"Enjoying your walk today?"

"Funny."

"How long have you been up here?" She continued to maneuver, bracing her backside against the granite. Her helmet bumped and scraped against the stone. She got under the rock.

"More than an hour. I came out early to hike and decided to take the rocks for a better work out. I slipped. Then that blasted rock fell and wedged me in. I couldn't pull out of the way in time as I slid down." He pushed against the rock wall with his right forearm and grimaced.

"You sure it isn't broken?"

His heart warmed at her concerned expression, remembering how close they had come to being married.

"I think it's a bad sprain at this point, my hiking boot is helping, but much longer and I think my ankle might snap. The pain's increasing." Steve's face hurt from frowning.

"Once they get the harness down to you, I'll push the rock while you try to pull your foot free if you can handle the pain. If this doesn't work, we'll have to get the saw or else the explosives." She gave him a lopsided grin.

"Hilarious. Do what you can."

"You must have wanted out of class this week."

"No, I'm getting my EMT. I'll get there if I

have to crawl. That is, if you get me out of here."

Two team members were on the rocks above him. "Hey, Steve." They lowered the harness. "Get this around you and buckle up. Let us handle your weight once they free you."

"Yeah, yeah, I know."

The straps slid against his back, allowing Steve to slip his arms into the loops. He cringed as he had to take an arm away from the wall of rock and pushed with his free leg for support. He pulled the straps around his thighs and buckled them. Each movement had to be quick so he wouldn't put prolonged pressure on the strained bones. It hurt so bad he didn't dare stress it more than necessary.

Who would have thought he'd be on this side of a rescue? He fumbled with the fastener and attached the two loops at his chest. "All right, let's get on with this." His lips pressed tight against each other, his jaw clenched so hard his teeth hurt, knowing he was in for some intense pain as Ronnie freed his foot.

~*~

Ronnie had done a good job of avoiding Steve the last few years. Oh, it was inevitable that they'd be on some calls together. But did she have to be the one to rescue him? She straightened her shoulders to steel herself against the emotions of the past. She had to be professional. Forget that she had fallen in love with him until…she choked back the thought.

Ronnie reached up and squeezed her gloved hand through the gap where Steve's foot was trapped. Another foothold allowed her the leverage needed as she applied gentle, but firm pressure on the soccer ball-*sized rock, yet her muscles strained at the effort. "OK Steve, see if you can pull your foot out."

"Ow, ow, ow."

"We're getting there Steve, keep trying." She continued to apply force.

He let out a determined yell.

The rock raised as his foot escaped and then settled back among the fallen stones. She kept her hand against the cold surface.

Steve held the foot out away from the rocks, the harness holding his weight. His face was scrunched in obvious pain.

She winced in sympathy. "OK guys, lower away. Steve, are you going to be able to put weight on that?"

"Man, I don't think so. I can feel it swelling. I've got to get this boot off soon."

Ronnie backed out of the gap.

Troy pushed his way in. "Let me get under him, Veronica. I want to be the one to help him out of this mess." Troy laughed.

Steve groaned.

She sent her best warning look at the arrogant rookie. "It's Ronnie—not Veronica."

Steve made the effort to keep his leg raised and used the other foot and his arms to keep from banging into the rocks.

The men above lowered him slowly.

Troy guided and pulled Steve away from the rock face.

As they settled him on the ground, Ronnie grabbed the medical kit, undid the latches, and found the wrap and splint material. "We'll get this boot off and splint you up."

George began to work at the laces of Steve's hiking boot, careful to keep the ankle straight.

"Yeah. Just get me out of here. I'm pretty sure I've been sufficiently humbled."

Troy stood next to him, a sadistic expression on his face. "Oh, I don't think so. How about this? Ever think of staying on the kiddie trails? Maybe you should get some glasses so you can see where you're going. You better stick to running into burning buildings. It's safer. Or how 'bout this thought? We now get to strap you into the Stokes basket and haul your sorry backside out of here."

"That's enough, Troy." Ronnie glared at the arrogant man. "You're supposed to be a professional. Knock it off so we can get him down to the ambulance. Help me pack up the equipment." She stood up next to the Stokes. The cupped light-weight wire basket would allow them to carry Steve through the woods down to the parking lot where the ambulance waited.

As they belted him in, Steve groaned again. "My SUV is at the trailhead."

George continued attaching the straps. "Don't worry about your vehicle. Maybe Ronnie can pick it up for you later."

"I..." she sputtered.

"You're off duty soon. Help him out and get his car."

The team traded off in carrying him on the narrow trail a mile from the lot.

Ronnie followed behind. The last thing she wanted was more time with Steve. She sighed heavily. He did need help. Great.

Nearing the last quarter mile, Troy handed off to another man on the front of the basket. He turned and walked backward, ribbing Steve. His heel caught on a root, sending him to the ground. He landed in a pile of fresh horse dung.

George chuckled. "You are not riding in my vehicle."

2

X-rays showed no fractures. Relieved, Steve waited for his release papers.

A hand slapped against the loose curtain surrounding the exam area. "Knock, knock." Her beautiful face peeked around, but her forehead held tight lines. "Can I come in?"

"Hey, Ronnie. Sure, come on in. Just waiting for the doctor to sign me out."

She did not look happy to be here. "Anything broken?" she asked.

"Nope. Just my pride."

"Oh, good." She laughed.

He loved her laugh. All the years he'd known her, that laugh lingered in his mind. She still wore khakis and hiking boots, but her light-colored hair hung free about her shoulders. Her bangs brushed across her eyebrows. "Not what you had on your agenda today?" That sweet voice lilted up to the ceiling.

"No, this kind of adventure, I don't need. You off duty?"

"Yeah, just finished my shift, so since George volunteered me...I thought I'd give you a lift home."

Nope, she was definitely not happy about

this. She most likely couldn't find anyone else to pass the task on to. She never wanted to be around him anymore. He'd have to thank George. "Sorry you got stuck with that. I don't think I'll be driving for a couple days."

She sighed heavily. Her arm rose up and she smacked her hand against her thigh. "I'll get your SUV. My brother's at my place for a few days. We'll pick it up and get it to your place after I get you settled. What about class this week? Will you be able to go?"

Could that be hope he saw in her eyes? Nah, probably not. "Oh, yeah. I'll make it. I'd appreciate the help."

"Glad to rescue you. Twice today." Again her beautiful laugh.

"Are you really?" Steve got off the gurney and attempted to hobble toward her, clumsy with the stiff padded boot protecting his injured foot.

Ronnie sat in the chair in the corner of the curtained room.

Steve fought the urge to hug her. A sigh escaped him as he realized it had just gotten cold in the room.

"So..." She reached over to snoop in the drawer of the cabinet next to her. "How long do you have to stay off the foot?"

"Doc said I have to stay in the boot and use the crutches for a week then see how it does. I guess I won't be running into any burning buildings this week." Oh, man, why did he say that? How stupid could he get?

Her eyebrows lifted. Sadness played over her face.

When would he think prior to opening his mouth?

She gave a half-hearted smile. "Well, that's good. I won't have to rescue you again."

"What will you do with your time?"

The nurse came in with the discharge papers and a pair of crutches. "You're all set to go. Here's a prescription for pain reliever. You'll need to take this for a few days with meals to keep the swelling down. The boot will help it to stay stabilized. Elevate the foot and ice it often."

"Yep. I know the drill."

"All right. Here are your crutches." The nurse handed them to him. "Unless you'd like a ride in a wheel chair."

Steve cocked his head and took the crutches from her. "No, my pride can't handle any more abuse."

Ronnie chuckled. "Are you sure? I'll be glad to wheel you out to the car." Her eyebrows wiggled up and down.

"I bet. No, crutches are good."

Ronnie took the paperwork and moved to his side.

A light citrus scent reached his nose. His senses were fully aware of her nearness as he swung himself down the hall.

She helped him settle into the passenger's seat of her truck. He could get used to her attention, even if only for a short time. He buckled up while she got in on the driver's side.

She drove out of the hospital parking lot.

After a few minutes of silence, Steve caught himself staring at her. "I really do appreciate your help today. We haven't had many calls together for a while. I've been wondering how you were doing. "

"Oh, I'm good. Keeping busy. Mom needs a lot of help these days." She kept her eyes on the road. "She's moving into a condo in a couple months. My days off usually consist of helping her sort through things."

"That must be challenging."

"Yeah. I think the move will do her good though. Take a step back from the memories. I think I'm having a harder time about her leaving the old house. But it's too much for her. Without Dad around anymore..." her words fell away.

Steve noticed the catch in her breath. "I think your Dad's becoming a legend, you know."

She took in a ragged breath. "He was an amazing man."

"The guys still stop by his photo at the department and talk about what he did."

Ronnie shifted in her seat.

"That was my first fire call. John's lucky to be alive."

"At least he is." Her words had a sharp edge.

Steve caught himself. "Sorry." His guilt freshened.

Her face contorted a bit. "Nature of the

profession. We all know the dangers."

"That we do."

They grew quiet again. Ronnie rested her elbow against the door frame; her fingers massaged her forehead and temple.

Steve regretted delving into the subject of her father. Not a bright decision on his part. Once again, he forgot to think first.

~*~

When were these memories going to become tolerable? It had been three and a half years since Ronnie's dad died saving John Jacobson from a burning house. She thought back to the day the chief arrived to break the news to her mom, her, and Adam.

Her father had been the number two man on the hose for the first attack team. Her dad had complained about John's ego and how he always wanted to be the hero.

Ronnie couldn't tolerate arrogance on the job from anyone anymore.

Steve had been there. Why couldn't he…no, she wasn't going there again.

Ronnie and Steve were so close back then. Best friends with the promise of something more, a relationship that might have led to marriage. He'd been her rock during the funeral. She broke up with him after things had settled down. She couldn't stand the thought of someday losing him in a similar way.

When she found out he had been third man on the hose outside, feeding it along, she couldn't help but wonder if he could have done something to save her father. The captain ordered him back since he was a rookie. But what if he could have saved her dad? Couldn't he have broken protocol? She sighed again as she turned into Steve's driveway.

His cabin sat against the backdrop of a pine-covered hillside. A small stream, flanked by blue spruce trees, meandered across the property behind the house, flowing toward the road and eventually disappearing into the culvert.

The beautiful scene settled down the heartbreak she had been reliving in her mind. She pulled to a stop as close to the door as possible. "Here you are." She put the truck in park and jumped out. The delightful smell of pine filled the air. She ran around the front to help him out.

Steve opened his door, set the ends of the crutches on the ground, slid on the seat and scooted out.

Ronnie touched his elbow and felt a delightful chill run through her. No, no...no feelings allowed. She shrugged it away. "I'll get you inside, and then go pick up my brother so we can get your vehicle. I can pick up your prescription, too, if you want."

"You know...I have pain reliever inside. That'll work fine." He made his way to the front stoop hobbling in front of her.

"You're pretty good with those crutches.

My guess is you've had some experience on them."

Steve laughed. "You could say that." He reached in his pocket for his keys.

She stayed behind him, her arm reached out toward him in case he stumbled. But she couldn't touch him, not again.

He unlocked it, and then handed the keys to her, pointing out the one for his car. He limped into the living room.

"What can I do for you before I take off?"

"There's an ice pack in the freezer. Can you grab it and a small towel from the drawer by the sink?" He took the crutches in one hand and hopped around to sit on the couch.

"Sure." She made certain he could sit down safely before heading into the kitchen. When she came back, she put a pillow under his leg, helped him open up the boot, put the ice pack in place, and then headed for the door. "I'll be back in half an hour, maybe forty-five minutes."

"Great, thanks again."

"No prob. Behave yourself."

~*~

Steve settled in on the couch, grabbed the remote, and turned on a baseball game. His mind couldn't stay on the game. The lulls in the play allowed his mind to drift back to Ronnie. He missed her. He missed them. The time they dated settled his life, readying him for that big leap.

Then her dad died and she broke it off. The guilt ate at him. He tried to get her to go out again, but she refused him every time. Not that he gave up easy, but all the guys at the station knew she refused to date firefighters from that point on. He still had the ring tucked safely away in his dresser. He hadn't been able to turn off his love for her as easily as she had for him.

With eyes closed, his mind took him back seeing the fire engulfed home. Being the rookie, he fed the hose that John and Ronnie's dad took into the inferno. He had never been that close to a large fire before. As they sprayed, a lot of smoke poured out of the door they had entered. When the smoke slowed and the hose didn't move, Steve hollered the information to the captain. He started to run for the door to help, but the captain ordered him back.

The second attack team headed in. They found John and Frank ten feet in. When they carried Frank out, Steve knew. Frank did not look good. The air mask was gone from its position on his face.

He shook his head and popped his eyes open to stop seeing it. Again. He couldn't have done anything, so why did he feel so guilty about it? *Lord, it's so hard. Please remove my guilt. I need to move on from it. Hurting my foot hasn't been a fun experience, but if it gives me another chance to try and get Ronnie to forgive me, then I'm all for it.*

An inning later, he heard the gravel crunching outside the door.

When she knocked, she announced them as she opened it.

"Come on in."

"We're back. Your car's home." Ronnie stepped in with her brother close behind.

"Hey man, how are ya?" Adam walked over and extended his hand. "Good to see you again. It's been a while. I hear my little sis got you out of a pickle today."

Steve leaned over and reached to shake Adam's hand. "Yeah, my luck."

"Can I make you a sandwich or something so you don't have to get up later?" Ronnie thumbed toward the kitchen.

"You know…that would be great. There's a bottle of water in the fridge and the pain reliever is up in the cupboard by the stove if you could. That'd save me some hobbling."

"Got it." She spun around fast and headed for the kitchen. Her hair, light as feathers, flew up in the air.

Adam looked at the television and sat on the chair next to the couch. "Still no score, huh?"

"No, it's a slow game today. Thanks for helping get my car."

"Oh, sure. You're still with the fire department, aren't you? How long have you been on there?"

"Just under four years. A little longer than your sister's been on rescue. We've ended up on a number of calls together. She's made for the job."

"Yeah, she decided long ago to be like

Dad. She loves the rescue work as much as he liked fire."

"Your dad's memory is really respected down at the station."

"Good to know." Adam's gaze stayed glued on the game.

Ronnie came back and put the items on the coffee table. The sandwich was wrapped in plastic. "There you go. I found a bag of chips, too. I know you like your potato chips. Anything else?"

"No, thanks. I'll be fine. This helps." He decided not to ask her to stay right there so he could just stare at her.

She pulled his car keys out of her pocket and set them on the table. "We're only a phone call away." She seemed to hesitate. "I...could pick you up for class Tuesday night if you can make it. I'm sure you'd rather not drive with that thing on your foot."

"That'd be great. Thanks." That offer must have been hard for her.

Adam headed for the door. "I'm in town for the week. I can help you out if you need something. It would get me out of the girlie room at Ma's." He smirked at his sister as she punched his arm. "What? You've loaded my old room with packed boxes. I don't like pink, OK?" He laughed, ducked and darted out the door before he got slugged again.

"Thanks for everything, Ronnie. I really do appreciate it."

"I know. You're welcome. I'll give you a call later and check in on you."

She closed the door and her lovely face disappeared, but not from his mind. He sighed. He closed his eyes and tried desperately to keep the vision of her before him. He smiled at the thought of her picking him up for training. More time together, cool.

His thoughts went to happier times. They had a lot of fun together. When her dad died, everything changed. She broke the news of splitting up with him two days after the funeral. No matter what he said, she stood her ground. He regretted telling her about being third man, but he had to tell her the whole story. She needed to know. She wanted to know. He wished he could have gone in the second that hose stopped moving. But endangering his own life and adding another to rescue wouldn't have helped anyone.

After spending most of this day with her around, his thoughts drifted to her creamy skin and pink lips. How he longed to press his own lips against hers again. Feel his arms around her slender body with her arms wrapped around him.

"*Arg.* I need a nap." He slid down further on the couch resting his head on the pillow, turned the game up a little louder and soon fell asleep.

3

How dumb could she be? Driving toward his house, she mentally beat herself up. Her heart remained so raw when it came to Steve. What possessed her to offer him a ride to class? Dumb. Let him find his own way. Who was she kidding? She couldn't just let him drive himself there with his leg braced up. She knew he would, but she had to go by his place on the way to the station. She had no excuse. No, she had to offer. She could do this. She could keep her emotions at bay. She'd let her feelings go years ago. Didn't she? Their relationship ended. She could just be a friend. Couldn't she?

Maybe Steve could have helped her father. Not much of a future with that looming in her mind. He knew that something had gone wrong in the burning house. He could have broken the rules. But what if he had died along with her dad?

No. He could have done something. She was sure of it.

Besides that, Jeannie confided in her that she liked Steve. She'd just joined the department a year ago and didn't really know their history.

Ronnie encouraged Jeannie to pursue Steve.

If that worked out, then he'd stop bugging her to get back together.

She wouldn't do it. Not with any firefighter, and especially not with Steve.

~*~

Five-thirty. She'd be here soon. He'd been anxious to get the training started to become an Emergency Medical Technician, but now that Ronnie said she'd drive, even better. Maybe this would give them the opportunity to move on. To start over.

Steve liked the physical side of firefighting, but he wanted to do more to help the injured. Medical stuff fascinated him anyway. The department had developed the policy that all firefighters must be EMT's as well. They responded to all rescue calls, so he understood the reason. The training didn't cost him anything.

And now it meant more time with Ronnie. He figured she wouldn't be too happy about the time together. But maybe…

She pulled into the driveway.

He stepped out and waved as she came to a stop near the stoop. The smile lighting her face turned his knees to water. Good thing he still needed crutches.

"How's the foot doing?" She stepped out to open the passenger door.

"Getting better every day. Thanks for driving tonight, though."

"No problem. Glad to help, Gimpy."

He loved that cheeky smirk of hers.

He hobbled into the department's training center, Ronnie close behind. The conference room had a dozen tables for two. He took the chair to the outside so he could stretch his leg out. Only a few more days in the boot. At least he hoped. He couldn't wait to get rid of the confining contraption.

"I've been waiting for this training to be offered again. It'll be good to get beyond First Responder status." She set her notebook down and took the seat next to him.

"It's required for the fire now, but I've wanted to do this for a while. I'm glad we're taking it together."

More classmates came into the room and found seats.

Jeannie, the only current female firefighter, took a seat in front of them.

Steve nodded to her.

She turned in her seat facing them. "Hi Ronnie, Steve. How's that foot doing?"

"It's good. How are you doing, Jeannie?"

She smiled and tipped her head. "I'm doing great. I was hoping you'd be able to make it to class."

"Yeah, Ronnie picked me up."

"Oh. I could have come by to get you."

"She has to drive by my place anyway. It worked out."

Jeannie's smile disappeared. "Ah." She

turned forward and opened her notebook.

~*~

Ronnie smiled and turned her attention to her own notebook. Why were men so clueless? Maybe she could arrange for Jeannie to pick him up if he needed a ride next time. Jeannie was trying so hard to get Steve to notice her. Men.

If Ronnie pushed a little, maybe that would convince him to look at Jeannie. She was strong, capable, quite attractive, and loved firefighting. It'd be good for him to get interested in someone else.

Ronnie had no future with him. Did she? No, definitely not. Ronnie had managed to avoid being around him, until now. But she had to help him. Didn't she? She glanced at him. Oh, that smile. She sighed.

"You OK?"

"Huh, oh, yeah. Just...anxious to get started."

The tall instructor walked into the dingy white room, much to her relief. He never said hello, just started to explain while walking in how tonight's class would be an overview of taking vitals. He passed out kits to half the class.

Ronnie felt Steve's gaze on her as the lesson began.

The instructor sat up front. "Since most of you are paired up at a table, you already have your new partner. Those of you sitting alone, find someone to pair up with."

Hoo, boy. Here she sat, next to the partner she didn't want to be a partner with. In more ways than one.

Jeannie looked back with a longing expression.

Steve adjusted his chair to face her more. He grinned. That expression would surely do her in. The instructor explained half of them were to take vitals, pulse, blood pressure, breathing, while the other half worked with the CPR manikins. "Do you want to check me first?"

Ronnie slid her chair around. "Sure." She suppressed a sigh. She caught Jeannie's glance. Ronnie should have found a way for Steve to sit with Jeannie. She couldn't get out of it now.

He rolled up his sleeve. Oooh, what a bicep. She remembered that strong arm around her, holding her tight. Comforting her. Ronnie's fingers trembled as she smoothed the blood pressure cuff around his arm to attach the Velcro. Why…was…she…shaking like this? *Come on girl, snap out of it.* She'd taken hundreds of pressures over the years. It's not like he was the first guy she'd checked. She put the ear pieces of the stethoscope in and concentrated on listening. His tight, muscular, tanned arm lay there in front of her. She closed her eyes to concentrate better. She finished, reached up to remove the device from her ears and pulled to release his arm from the contraption. "One ten over seventy." She looked up. Their gazes locked for the briefest moment and it transported her to another time. A happier time.

What is wrong with her? This was no time for memories. She reached to take his pulse. As she held her middle and ring finger against the rhythm, she could have sworn the pace picked up. Knowing she should check his breathing while taking the pulse, she watched the rise and fall of his chest. His...well-defined...chest. "Running close to a hundred Steve. That's a bit high. Respirations about twenty."

"You got me all twitter pated." Steve grinned again.

Jeannie looked at them with a puzzled, shocked expression.

Ronnie's heart sunk a bit.

She couldn't look at Steve. "I haven't heard that line since I was a kid."

"Facts are facts."

Heat rose in her cheeks. Why didn't she think to wait for Jeannie? She didn't want to fall for him, but she stood on the edge of that precipice, all the while feeling her balance waver. "All right, your turn." She held her arm out as he picked up the pressure cuff.

~*~

Steve wrapped the nylon piece around her slender, toned arm. Finding a normal pressure, he placed his fingers against her wrist. She looked away as he counted the respirations in the rise and fall of her chest. He glanced up as her face turned rosy then looked back down. He had to retain a professional attitude. He had to follow the protocol for respirations on anyone. The longest thirty seconds he'd had for a while. "Appears you're normal. That's a good thing. Surprising, but good."

He ducked as Ronnie gave him a playful slap.

The class switched stations so Steve and Ronnie took their places next to the CPR manikin.

Even though he could perform CPR in his sleep, the constantly changing guidelines required that he stay on top of all the updates.

The training went well.

For the fifteen minute break, they slipped on their jackets and he followed her outside to a picnic area next to the training center. She held the door for him. The temperatures weren't bad for fall. The sun had already slipped behind the surrounding foothills, so the evening chill settled in.

~*~

"What do you think of the class so far?" She took a drink, and then sat down at the picnic table with her back leaning against the hard, cold edge. She pulled two snack bars out of her coat pocket and handed one to Steve.

"Thanks. Hey, our old hiking snacks. I love these." Steve unwrapped the familiar favorite and took a bite. "Class is good. The instructor seems very experienced. I think it'll be good." He sat next to her, leaned the crutches against the table, raised the clunky boot to the bench, and leaned forward with his elbows on his knees.

"Yeah, me, too. I'm glad I finally got the ball rolling for my EMT." Her gaze stayed fixated on the silhouetted pine trees dotting the area.

"So…I was thinking. Maybe we could do dinner one of these nights."

Ronnie glanced at him.

The dim street light illuminated the hopeful look in his eyes.

"Steve…" she paused as she thought of how she could word this. She hated to hurt anyone's feelings, but she had to protect the barrier over her heart. "You know I don't date firefighters any more. I just can't handle the stress."

"I know." He lowered his head and looked down at his intertwined fingers. "I miss…us. What can I say? Listen, Ronnie. It's no secret I still really like you. I've never stopped. I just want to spend more time with you. No strings attached."

"More time means getting closer. It's hard enough in class. I don't think I can risk any more right now, Steve. I can't bear the thought of going through what my mother went through when Dad died. It's just too hard."

"I don't plan on dying. You need to trust

the Lord with these worries. Why stop yourself from enjoying a relationship because of fear?"

"Steve, we've been through this. And you don't know if you'll die." She looked away, her heart crashing again at the memory of when she had broken off their relationship. He might have been able to do more for her dad, but she couldn't voice that to him. Logic told her he couldn't have, but her heart wouldn't accept it. Even though she had grown accustomed to the thought of maybe spending her life with him, it would become a life of fear and resentment. What if he didn't make it out someday? What if he really could have saved her father, and didn't? Losing her father still tore at her gut. They'd been so close. She missed him so much. Tears threatened to cross the threshold that she tried so hard to block.

Steve always had to bring up the "trust God" card.

She used to trust God. But now…how could she trust a God who allowed her father to die doing something so heroic? Her dad would have tried to keep John from going further into the fire. But John's overconfidence kept him pushing them forward until he had sucked all the air out of his tank. Then the wall fell on them both, knocking John out and his mask off.

Her dad broke a cardinal rule by putting his mask on John as he attempted to save the man. Then part of the ceiling came crashing down and debris blocked the path of escape. Her dad had been able to drag John near the door where they were found. Dad died on the way to the hospital. He had breathed in too much of the toxic smoke for too long. How could she trust the same thing wouldn't repeat itself? No, trust in a God like that would not be something she'd be doing anytime soon.

She had to admit, rejecting Steve would be so much easier if he weren't so handsome, and kind…and giving…and a gentleman…and exactly what she wanted in a husband. Shaking her head, she sighed and crossed her arms. She had to find a way to push him toward Jeannie. To push him away.

"I'm sorry. I know. I'll let it go. But…just know I'm here if you change your mind." His eyebrows wiggled.

It made her snicker.

"No hard feelings?"

"No, no hard feelings. We should get back inside." If these times continued she would fall into a danger zone she didn't want to enter. She would have to spend breaks with others. Maybe she could encourage Jeannie to come along. Yeah, that would give her the opportunity to push them together.

"Hey, I bet Jeannie could take you home tonight." Ronnie tried the suggestion as she held the door open for him.

"That would be silly. She lives in the opposite direction. You have to drive right by my house on your way home. You trying to get rid of me?"

"No, no. I...uh...just thought you might...never mind." What could she possibly say here? *Jeannie likes you. Go be with her.* Deep down she didn't really want to push them together no matter how much she tried to convince herself that her feelings for him were gone.

After class, they got in her truck and she turned on the radio, hoping it would distract any uncomfortable conversation on the ride home.

The oldies country station blared out a song about falling in love.

She quickly changed the station. She would not go there in her mind.

4

The pagers screamed out the emergency tone. As the sound ended, the dispatcher's voice came over the unit, indicating a car had hit an elk near mile marker four on County Road 65.

Steve jumped to his feet and headed for the truck.

Troy, Jeannie, and Carl responded to the call with him.

Several weeks had passed since his ankle injury, and he was glad to be working again.

Troy hit the lights and siren. The vehicle laptop displayed a map to the location. The rookie leaned forward against the shoulder strap, eyes fixed forward. His leg bounced at a frantic pace.

"I know you're excited, Troy, but remember, you have to keep it cool and do the job."

"Yeah, yeah, I know. Just get there." Troy's impetuous behavior tended to get him in trouble with the chief. If he continued, he wouldn't last with the department.

Steve didn't want him lose his job.

Rounding the curves, they saw a car in the ditch. An elderly woman stood on the side of the road, wringing her hands.

A police car, coming from the other direction, pulled in behind her.

The driver's side front end had smashed into a tree not far off the road. The car sat at a bit of an angle. The driver must have turned too sharp to avoid hitting the animal, which obviously didn't work.

The elk limped out in the field across the road trying to catch up to the herd. A few more of the large animals stood watching.

More sirens headed to the scene.

Steve parked the large truck, partially blocking the roadway.

Troy jumped out and raced toward the car with the Jaws of Life.

Steve caught up, fighting a slight, leftover limp.

The young man behind the wheel had blood oozing from a wound on his face and a dazed expression.

Carl went to check on the woman.

"Get out of the way," Troy yelled as he began to start up the Jaws.

"Troy, wait."

"We have to get him out. Get out of the way." He set the machine in the joint of the door.

"Troy. Stop. That isn't neces…"

The roar stopped him mid-sentence. Steve reached over and shut off the machine. He put a hand against Troy's chest and held it firm.

"What are you doing, man?"

Jeannie took the Jaws out of Troy's hands

and set it off to the side.

Steve reached out for the door handle and opened it. "Try it before you pry it, Troy."

Troy's face went instantly red.

"You can see the door isn't damaged, Troy," Jeannie said.

"All right. I get it." Troy stomped back.

Steve knelt next to the driver, "Sit tight. We'll get you out of here." He began an assessment of the guy's injuries.

"What...I didn't see...Oh, man...my car." He touched the bridge of his nose, saw the blood on his fingers and tried to get out of the car.

"Sit tight." Steve put his hands on the victim's shoulders. "You could have more injuries." He took hold of the back of the man's skull and placed his other hand under the chin, fingers bracing, holding firm in case of a neck injury. "Let the medics check you over."

A paramedic and Ronnie came down to the car.

Ronnie crawled in the passenger side. "What have you got, Steve?"

Peter, the paramedic, crawled in the backseat directly behind the driver and stabilized the victim's head from the sides, relieving Steve from his hold.

"Laceration on the nose. No other apparent injuries."

Ronnie separated the collar used to protect the neck. "What's your name?"

"Uh, Brandon." His eyes looked dazed.

"Do you know what day it is?"

He paused a minute, "Friday?"

"How old are you, Brandon?"

"Twenty-five."

"Brandon, we're going to get this collar on you just in case you have any neck injuries, then get you back-boarded and out of here."

"I'm fine. I can get out."

Steve placed a hand on the man's chest and the paramedic in the back seat shifted to keep a firm hold on Brandon's head, preventing further movement.

"Humor me. Let's just get you to the hospital and have you checked out." Ronnie slipped the front of the plastic collar on him, and then slid the back half into place working around the medics' hold. She nodded to Steve who attached it on the other side.

She checked his pupils for any further sign of a head injury. "So you found out elk rule the roads around here."

"It jumped out in front of me so fast..."

"I hate when they do that." She tended to the cut on the bridge of his nose. "Are you on any medications?"

Ronnie handled victims so well. She had a soothing presence and her humor helped to keep the patient at ease. She began to take his blood pressure, pulse and respiration, all the while speaking to Brandon in a calm voice.

Jeannie returned with the short board, and stood to the side ready to help if needed. She smiled so sweet at him.

The medic in the back seat continued to keep the patient's head stabilized as Jeannie slid the board behind him.

Ronnie assisted in connecting the straps to hold him to the board, one strap going across his forehead and allowing Peter to release his hold.

Peter backed out of the rear seat telling Ronnie, "Guide his legs as we get him on the long board."

The long board had already been positioned. They turned the victim to slowly lower him with the short board onto the long board. His upper body now stable, Ronnie aligned his legs.

The fire chief walked toward Steve, who now stood out of the way of the medics. George frowned at Troy, who hurried back to the truck carrying the Jaws. "What's up with him?"

"Troy was ready to cut the car up, but the door wasn't locked or damaged."

"Assuming you told him?"

"Yep. Try it before you pry it." Steve shrugged. "He forgot."

"When is it going to sink into him?"

"Give him some time. You know how long it takes with some probies. We were all excitable in our probationary stage."

"Keep me posted," George said. "Looks like they've got the vic ready."

Steve assisted in carrying the boarded patient up to the waiting ambulance.

As they closed the doors, Ronnie headed for her rig.

Steve caught up with her. "Good job back there, Ronnie."

"Oh, yeah, thanks. Thanks for the help, too. I...uh...have to go." The door closed and she was gone.

5

Ronnie had Friday off and headed over to help her mom pack up more of the house. She didn't really want to go through the stuff she hadn't taken to her apartment. But Mom had threatened to pitch it. She had no idea where she'd store it, even if she did keep it. "Mom? I'm here."

"Hey, sis." Adam finished taping the box in front of him. "Mom's upstairs."

"Hey, Adam. Thanks. I'll go up and help her." Ronnie headed up the wooden staircase nostalgically running her hand up the rail's smooth wood.

Dad had replaced the original black metal railing for the beautiful oak years ago. He had spent many hours sanding and varnishing it to make sure it would last. It would probably outlive the house. It warmed her heart and made her realize how much she'd miss the place.

"Mom?"

"In here, honey."

Dad's old office. She'd avoided his room all this time. Her mom sat on the floor with an open box beside her loading books off the lowest shelf. Ronnie stopped in the doorway.

"Hey, Mom, Adam could do this room…" She couldn't make the offer herself.

"Hi, sweetheart. No, I need to. I like to see your dad's things. I don't know why I've held onto them for so long. But now it's time. I thought I'd donate his woodworking books to the technical college. Unless you want any of them."

Ronnie sat down, crossed her legs and looked into the box. "No, I don't think so." She took a couple off the shelf and looked at the titles before putting them in the box. A heavy sigh escaped her lips. She'd always planned to be strong around her mom, but being here; around Dad's things…she wanted to be a little girl again. Back when he still sat in this room planning his next project.

Her mom took her hand, patting it with the other. "It's OK, honey." Mom fought apparent aching muscles to stand. Placing her hands on her lower back, she stretched. "How's your class going?"

Ronnie squeezed one more book into the box. "Oh, it's good. A lot to remember, but I'm loving it."

"And…" Her mom's eyebrow quirked up. "How's Steve?"

"Mom…"

"Just asking." Her hands went up in surrender. She grabbed a smaller box, moved over to a desk drawer and began to unload it. "He's a good man. I liked him. So did your dad."

"I know, Mom. But it's over. I'm not going

to date him. We're just stuck in the same class. Besides, there's another gal in the department who really likes him."

"Does he seem interested in this girl?"

"Oh, you know Steve. Well, men in general. I don't think he has a clue. She keeps trying to get his attention. But, he's all about the job."

"Unless it was you, I bet."

"Mom…"

"Could be a divine appointment that you are in that class with him."

"Doubtful. We're in the same town and both need the same class. That's all. I know what you're thinking. God did not put us together for this." She abruptly grabbed the tape gun, positioned it, pulled back fast, and sealed the box. The sharp noise felt like her heart ripping again. Time to cram those memories back down where they belonged. She marked the lid for the college and slid it across the hardwood floor out to the hallway. She wanted to follow the box out of the room, but she wouldn't leave the work to her mom.

Closing the drawer she just emptied, her mom grabbed her cup of coffee and leaned back in the brown leather chair. "Come sit for a minute." She pointed to the wing-backed chair in the corner.

"I just got here. We need to pack."

"Sit." Ah, the warning tone.

Ronnie flung herself into the chair, arms

draped over each padded arm. She slouched, legs stretched straight out, feeling as if she were twelve years old. She braced for the lecture coming.

"When are you going to forgive him for what he didn't do?"

Ronnie began picking her nails.

"Honey, the love of a good man is a gift. I'm afraid you've pushed away something potentially special in your life."

"Mom, I can't. The memory won't leave me. Steve was right there at the scene when Dad died. Right outside."

"You know he couldn't have done anything to help. Your dad made the decision he made. Maybe he's the one you should be mad at."

"That's not going to happen." She stood, wanting to run. Grabbing another box, she headed to the closet against the opposite wall and flung open the worn-out, wooden bi-fold doors.

Her mom helped her bring down a heavy box off the shelf.

"You know how much I loved your dad, right?"

"Yeah, I know." Ronnie looked into her mom's moistening eyes.

"For quite a while after the fire, I was so mad at your father."

"Mom…he died. How could you be mad at him? He couldn't help it." Pain filled Ronnie's chest upon hearing her mom's words.

"He knew better than to take off his mask.

I couldn't understand it. I had to think long and hard about it to reach a point of not being mad." She leaned a shoulder into the wall and lowered her gaze. "But after twenty-eight years of marriage, deep in my heart I knew why. He was a saver. A fixer. He wouldn't let John die on his watch. They were partners. He felt responsible."

"But if someone had gotten to them, maybe dad would still be alive."

"Someone...like Steve?"

Ronnie hated to admit to it out loud. It had been easier to just blame him inside herself. "Yes, like Steve. He knew something had happened in there."

"And he did what he had been trained to do. And you know he had to follow orders."

Ronnie plopped down, pushed into the closet, and leaned against the back wall, legs stretched out.

Her mom lowered down next to her. "Do you think I could have stopped loving him because he chose to be a fireman?"

"No."

"You're right. I loved the things about him that made him a firefighter. Even though I lost him way too soon, I never would have traded the life I had with him. We were blessed by a lot of happy years. Plus I got you and your brother out of the deal." She bent her head to look in Ronnie's eyes and smiled.

A tear ran down Ronnie's face. She pulled her sleeves over her hands and wiped at the errant moisture. Her mother raised her arm, pulled Ronnie close, and kissed the top of her head. Mom was so strong. Ronnie admired her ability to deal with the pain and loss.

"Where are you two?" Adam's voice boomed into the peace. "Oh sure. I'm down there working my tail off and you two are sloughing off up here."

Ronnie and her mom looked at each other and chuckled.

"Mom, are you sure he is a blessing to you?" She took an elbow to her ribs.

"We're on a break. Help me up." Her mom waved her hand in the air toward Adam.

He pulled her up.

"Let's go get a cup of coffee," Mom said. "We have to plan Thanksgiving with this move going on."

"Hey, Adam, take that box on your way." Ronnie pointed to the heavy book box and grabbed her mom by the crook of the elbow.

He grunted as he hefted it up in his arms.

She laughed.

6

It would be a long day with the snow whipping in dizzying circles outside the window. Blizzard conditions had begun quite suddenly as the storm front settled into the canyon. Whenever the upslope conditions presented like this, the foothills were hammered by snow. November didn't always see a lot, but this year was certainly the exception. Visibility had diminished to just ten feet.

The pager tone went off followed by the information of an accident.

Ronnie and her partner, Matt, headed out.

"Wow, this is getting bad. It came out of nowhere." Nerve endings skittered beneath Ronnie's skin.

The icy conditions could determine their own fate in the blink of an eye. The pavement was invisible as the snow blew low over the white road. It looked more like the end of the day rather than morning with the gloomy, heavy clouds. Large flakes of snow hit the windshield like small white daggers.

They neared the location and a familiar red car came into sight through the blustering snow.

Ronnie's heart squeezed.

Debra, Steve's mom, had bought the little sports car after her husband died. Her humorous bumper sticker was visible on the back of the vehicle, so there was no mistaking Debra's car. The woman had been like a second mom to Ronnie when she dated Steve.

They jumped out of the emergency vehicle.

Assessing the damage, it was easy to see the car hung partway over the embankment. It seemed to be precariously ready to slip down into the creek. The wind blasted against it coating the side with snow and it rocked with each gust.

Fear wrapped itself in Ronnie's heart. Where was the fire department?

They would need to tie off the vehicle with the winch on the big rig.

Far off sirens sounded and Ronnie breathed easier, but worry ate at her. The rig needed to hurry. The car didn't seem to have a decent purchase on solid ground. Ronnie pulled up the collar of her coat and rushed to the car.

Mrs. McNeal, eyes wide and body seemingly frozen in the seat, stared straight ahead.

"Don't move. Stay as still as you can. We have to get the wheels blocked."

The woman gripped the wheel tight with her gloved hands, barely willing to turn her head. Fear lived in her expression. She clutched a cell phone in her hand. The car shifted in the wind, being high-centered over the snow bank at the edge of the road.

A squeak escaped Debra's mouth. "Ronnie, help."

Ronnie could barely hear it through the closed window and the wind blowing. "We will." She managed to say through her constricted throat. "We'll get you out of this. Are you hurt?" Ronnie deflected the blowing snow from her eyes. The biting wind found every opening of her jacket to gain access to her skin. Shivers wracked her body and not just from the cold.

Mrs. McNeal was in serious danger.

"N-no. I don't think so. Every time I shift a little, it seems to slide more. I don't dare move."

"I know. Sit tight."

Matt worked at trying to block the wheels, but they only lightly touched the ground and every gust made it rise a little more. He took hold of the bumper and pulled it down. "Call in and tell them to step on it. We need the winch now. The bank is giving way and I'm not sure we can wait much longer."

Ronnie pulled out her radio explaining the level of urgency before signing off. "We've got to get her out of there."

"We can't risk it. If we make the move to open the door, her shifting weight will definitely send the car down to the creek."

As if the words caused a reaction, the car slid again, resulting in a loud shriek from inside the vehicle.

The sirens were drawing closer, but after their own harrowing ride, the big rig would have difficulty maneuvering the curves in the road of the canyon.

"Hurry up you guys..." Ronnie checked out the front end.

The car hung over the creek which was about fifteen feet below. Snow covered the embankment and slope, only a few rocks protruded through the white. There were no trees to stop a decent should the car let go, only scant brush. Hardly a match against a three-thousand-pound car. The front end hung in the air, rocking on the piled up snow. There'd be no way to brace it from going over.

"Oh, Ronnie." Debra began to cry.

"I know. We're trying to figure something out. I hear the trucks. They'll be here soon."

Matt kept his weight on the rear bumper.

Ronnie spotted a fallen log on the other side of the road. Kicking it free of the snow, she dragged it over to the car, thinking she could shore up the front end. Before she could even get the log in position, the car shifted and began to slide down the embankment.

"No!" Ronnie ran for the door handle in a futile attempt to keep it from going over the edge.

Debra's terror-stricken face filled the driver's side window, and she screamed as the car teetered.

Ronnie screamed, too, desperately trying to hold on to the door handle. It ripped from her fingers as three thousand pounds of steel tilted and then sliced through the knee-deep snow. The front end slammed against a rock, and, as if in slow motion, the car's back end flipped over on its roof, slid a few more feet, and came to a stop partly submerged in the icy creek.

Red lights bounced off the opposite hillside next to the creek.

Ronnie and Matt reached the upside down vehicle, dropped to the ground, and pulled at the piled up snow near the window. Ronnie could almost feel her heart being ripped out of her chest. Broken glass littered the ground around the car.

Firefighters swarmed down the embankment.

"Mom!" Steve yelled as he nearly rolled down the packed earth, his desperation evident as he stumbled over lumps and bumps buried under the snow.

Debra hung upside down by the seatbelt. Her arms dangled helplessly. A bit of blood ran on the side of her face into her hairline. The woman's hair was wet, and one gloved hand lay in the icy water. Her lolling head indicated she'd lost consciousness.

Matt and Ronnie couldn't get at her from the driver's side since it sat in the creek. The car door and frame were severely dented where the car had hit the rock, but with the glass gone, it allowed Ronnie to squeeze into the space. She pushed aside the spent air bags.

The roar of the Jaws of Life shattered the air.

"Mrs. McNeal? We're going to get you out of here." No answer. No movement. Ronnie pulled off her gloves and checked the woman's neck for a pulse. Feeling the rhythm thrust a sigh out of Ronnie's chest.

Matt flung a neck brace in and it hit her thigh.

She frantically worked at securing it around Debra. They would have to lower her soon.

Metal ripping behind Ronnie caused her to pull her legs in further and she shielded Debra from the popping and grinding. It seemed to take forever for the door to be removed and pulled out of the way.

Steve stuck his head in. "How is she?"

"Unconscious. We need to get her down. Get in here and hold her while I cut the seat belt."

Steve crawled in, hampered by his bulky turn-out coat. He lay on the roof, reaching for his mother's upper body so she wouldn't fall hard. Ronnie cut the belt, but Mrs. McNeal didn't drop. Her leg was caught between the steering wheel and the door panel.

Another firefighter stood in the water working the Jaws on the driver's door. As it separated, they were able to free Mrs. McNeal's leg and lower her down. The team operated together to get the woman onto the backboard and to remove her from the car.

A groan escaped Debra as her eyes opened.

"We've got you, Mom. You'll be OK." Steve encouraged her, but the fear was still evident in his expression.

Once out of the vehicle, they strapped Mrs. McNeal down. Several of them carried her toward the gurney stationed up on the road, Steve alongside them, holding his mother's hand. They had to trudge through the snow avoiding the hidden rocks, and passed Debra off to the next set of firefighters in more stable positions. Steve stayed by her side, blocking the blowing snow from hitting Debra's face with his gloved hand.

Ronnie sat back on her heels next to the upside down vehicle. Her chin hit her chest as she muttered, "It's all my fault."

Matt knelt next to her, placing his hand on her shoulder. "Don't blame yourself. That car would have gone over regardless. We couldn't have done any more. This is not your fault."

"I caused it to go over with that stupid log. This is my fault." She wept into her gloved hands. The screaming siren of the ambulance attested to the reality of what had happened. The beeping of the tow truck backing into position overtook the sound of the creek and her sobs.

Matt pulled her up by the arm. "Come on Ronnie. Let's go."

She struggled to her feet, guilt riddled her mind. Her vision blurred with the tears, making it difficult to maneuver up the rocky, snow covered slope. The rivulets seemed to freeze against her face. Snowflakes added to the moisture. She didn't want to go to the hospital to retrieve their backboard from the ambulance team. How would she be able to face Steve after what she'd done? Maybe Matt would go in. No, she would have to sign off, too. Face the music. Ronnie almost started praying, but stopped herself. *Mrs. McNeal just has to be OK.*

~*~

Steve stood outside the ER waiting for the doctor. He'd called his sisters from his cell. They wanted to fly out immediately, but he convinced them to wait until he found out how bad their mom's injuries were. Still in his turn-out gear, minus the heavy coat which over-filled one of the chairs, he paced in heavy boots, leaving small puddles on the floor. How long would he have to wait?

Mom had regained consciousness at the scene, but she hadn't been coherent.

Steve hoped her confusion would be temporary.

A nurse came through the doors. "Mr. McNeal?"

He rushed to her. "Yeah, here."

She held up her hand blocking him. "We're taking her to X-ray right now. As soon as she's back, we'll come get you."

"Is she OK? What did the doctor say?"

"The doctor will be out in just a minute to speak to you." Then she turned and went back the way she came.

Steve paced some more, looking through the small windows in the doors each time he passed. His boots clomped with each step.

A few minutes later, a woman in purple scrubs came out asking for him.

"Here." He rushed over to her.

"I'm Dr. Becky Jordan." She reached out to shake his hand.

"How's my mom?"

"She's stable. We've sent her to X-ray. I suspect her left leg is broken. I understand she lost consciousness?"

"Yes, she must have been knocked unconscious or passed out when her car went over the edge and rolled."

"I've ordered films of her head and neck as well. It'll be a bit before they bring her back up. I'll send someone out for you then. She is awake, but rather confused. Try to relax. We'll take care of her."

"Thank you, doctor." Steve ran his hand through his hair then slumped down into the chair next to his coat. The waiting room had about a half a dozen people in it. But there was no one for him to lean on, except One. He rubbed his whisker stubble and bowed his head. "Father, please be with her. Give the doctors wisdom in treating her. I pray that she will be all right." He choked up. The words could no longer come.

The automatic doors opened.

Matt and Ronnie came in.

He jumped out of the chair. He needed someone to hold. He reached out, but she stopped and stepped back.

~*~

"How is she?" Ronnie couldn't look him in the eyes.

Worry lines creased his face. "They're running X-rays on her right now. I haven't seen her yet. The doctor said she's pretty sure mom's leg is broken."

Ronnie turned away.

"Is there anything we can do?" Matt put a hand on Steve's shoulder.

"No, thanks. Just have to wait. I want to see her for myself."

Guilt washed over Ronnie like a waterfall. Each pang of fault dropped to another level of responsibility, beating it harder into her. If only...

Steve and Matt took chairs across from her.

She barely heard Matt talking about the accident.

"The car teetered with every gust of wind. I've never seen anything like it." Matt shook his head.

Ronnie closed her eyes in a vain attempt to keep the tears from escaping, fighting the urge to cover her ears. But the movie of the car going over played against her eyelids. She popped them back open.

"She shouldn't have been out with this weather moving in. Sometimes her independence drives me crazy." Steve pounded his hand on the chair.

"You know how these storms can move in. It iced over fast when the wind started."

"Yeah, I know, but still. The forecast said the chances were pretty good. What was she thinking?"

"This isn't her fault!" Ronnie's control broke. She stood and nearly ran to the ladies room, knowing she was the one who should be blamed.

~*~

Steve looked back at Matt. "What's wrong with Ronnie?"

"She's feeling guilty. We were doing everything we could to keep your mom's car from going over. The back tires weren't even on the ground and the front end hung halfway over, so I tried to put my weight on the back bumper. Ronnie grabbed a section of a downed tree to try to block the front end, but the way it balanced at an angle on the snow bank, it would have gone over no matter what we did. I felt it slipping away from me even before she tried to use that log to block the tires. We had no time."

"I have no doubt you guys did everything

you could."

"I know. But Ronnie feels like she's responsible for the car pitching over. I tried to tell her it was going over anyway, but she won't listen."

"That's ridiculous."

A nurse came through the doors. "Steve McNeal?"

"Yeah, here." Steve hurried over to her.

"She's back from X-ray. I'll take you to her now."

Matt called out, "Let us know how she is."

Without looking back, Steve waved as he rushed after the nurse.

7

Class attendance was light the week of Thanksgiving, so they did mostly review. Ronnie was relieved. Concentrating on complex problems was beyond her these days. Dealing with her mistake ripped her up inside. What could she have done differently? If only…

Steve wasn't there, thankfully. She couldn't face him yet.

Jeannie sat by herself at a middle table.

"Hi, Jeannie. Can I sit with you?"

"Hi, Ronnie, sure. Have a seat."

"Thanks." Ronnie sat and flipped through her notebook.

"How are you doing?" Jeannie's brow creased.

"OK, I guess. How 'bout you?"

"I'm good. I suppose Steve won't make it tonight." Her glance, ever hopeful, scanned the room. "I heard he took some time off to take care of his mom."

"Yeah, I suppose."

"Why the look?"

"Oh, nothing. I just wish they didn't have to go through what happened. I wish I'd have done things differently."

Jeannie put a hand on Ronnie's arm. "She'll be OK. What else could you have done? It was a tough situation. It seemed like a good idea. I might have done it myself."

"I can't think about it anymore. So tell me...have you been able to get Steve's attention yet?"

"No. I'm not sure it's worth it. He's nice and all, certainly nice on the eyes, but he never bites when I throw out my line."

"That sounds like him. Typical guy. Maybe you should just ask him out?" A funny catch occurred in Ronnie's heart when the words left her mouth. She had to keep pushing those two together. Anything to prevent her from getting any closer to him. Especially now. Surely he wouldn't even consider seeing her after she made such a stupid mistake and risked the life of his mother.

It proved nearly impossible to keep her mind on the topic of class. Thankful it had been overview, she could always study it again later.

~*~

Thanksgiving Day. Every year since her dad died made it hard for Ronnie to feel thankful. For her mom's sake, she put on her happy face. Ronnie was glad she didn't have to work the holiday since she couldn't seem to get her groove back for the job. Would she ever feel capable of this work again? Her mind seemed intent on playing her failure over and over again. She hadn't seen Steve either, which didn't make her guilt ease. During the class Monday, she hid her edginess, wondering if he'd walk in late. Any ability to concentrate was shot. Probably a good thing since she had no idea what she would say to him. An apology seemed so shallow. *Hello, Steve. Sorry I almost killed your mother with my negligence...*

Her family held Thanksgiving at her apartment since her mom's house was packed up. They would move Mom's things to the condo the next day.

"Have you heard how Debra is?" Her mom washed her hands after placing the turkey roaster in the oven.

"Not really. I get updates from the guys at the station." A deep sigh escaped Ronnie's chest. "Steve hasn't been around."

"You didn't call?"

"No."

Her mom leaned against the counter as she dried her hands on a couple of paper towels. Then she gave "the look."

Ronnie turned away to prevent it from boring into her brain.

A hand touched her shoulder, gentle and comforting. "Honey...the accident isn't your fault."

"Yes it is, Mom. If I hadn't tried to shove a log under the front end..."

"You tried to save her. You did the best

you could given the circumstances."

"If I had waited for the truck...they pulled up just as the car went over. They could have tied it off. I should have helped Matt hold it down. Steve had to have seen it go over." Her hands flew up, agitating in the air. "Can you imagine seeing that happen to your mother? And there I stood, helpless to stop what I caused."

"You can't torture yourself like this. Things happen. We can't always stop the bad things. Come on. Let's go sit down and have a cup of coffee. Adam will be here soon." Her mother refilled their cups. Handing Ronnie one, she motioned toward the couch.

They sat quiet for a while.

Ronnie's eyes fixated on the ceramic pilgrims positioned on her coffee table.

Her mom reached out and picked up a figurine. "Can you imagine coming to a new world, raising a family in an untamed land?" She turned the figure around in her fingers. "I wonder how many struggled with feeling as if they made a mistake sailing across the ocean, hoping to start a new life. They couldn't go back. Encountering Indians, hunger, disease, uncertainty..."

The topic puzzled Ronnie.

"When your dad died, I had to start a new life. I had no choice. I couldn't change what had happened. I had to move on. As much as I didn't want to at first, I had to. I also had to come to terms with his decision to do what he did. I couldn't change that, either. Sometimes you have to accept the fact that it is what it is, and you have to deal with it."

"I could have killed her." Tears drizzled down Ronnie's cheeks.

"But you didn't. She'll get through this. So will you, but you have to forgive yourself." Her mom scooted over and wrapped an arm around Ronnie's shoulders.

"I'm so tired of crying over this. How can I ever expect to be a professional at this job when it wears me down like this?"

"Your dad felt the same way in the beginning. When he started out as a rookie, he would come home and talk about how hard it was to remember all of the training techniques."

"Dad struggled?"

"Oh, yes. It takes practice. Then every situation is different, so you all have to be so flexible in decisions. There's no right answer for everything that happens. And the harder the call, the more emotions you have to deal with. Your situation right now is tough. Your dad had a difficult time, too."

A knock hit the door. "That must be Adam. We better get the rest of this dinner started." Her mom let him in.

"When do we eat? I'm starved."

"Not for three hours or so, you better have a donut." Ronnie pointed to the pastry box on the table.

~*~

"I don't need to go to class." Steve flipped the eggs over. He always made a big breakfast on Saturdays.

"Yes you do. You've skipped one already, and I know how bad you want to get your EMT. So go. I'm tired of your hovering." Steve's mom winked at him. "I'll be fine."

"All right. But I'm coming back right after it's done."

"Only if you bring me a treat."

"Pistachio ice cream?"

"Of course."

"What if they don't have it?"

"Then there's no reason to go in there." His mom only half teased about her ice cream choice.

He climbed in his jeep and leaned his head against the headrest for just a minute. Exhaustion slapped him upside the head as he drove off to class in the darkness. The first couple of days were the hardest when he had to wake her every couple of hours due to the concussion.

He'd been off work for a week now, fixing things for her, cooking, cleaning. She managed to get around pretty good on the crutches now, but he wanted to stick around to help. Her concussion had been mild, but he still worried.

He should have called Ronnie. He'd been so absorbed in taking care of his mom and making sure she healed up that he just didn't think about it at the right time. She'd be at class so he could talk to her there.

Steve went through the propped open door and stood just inside scanning the room.

Ronnie would have to hurry or she'd miss the start of class.

Troy raised a hand in greeting.

Steve groaned a bit inside, and walked over to him. "Hey, Troy."

"Hey, man. How goes it?"

"Great. Mom's on the mend. So…" he looked around again. "Have you seen Ronnie?"

"No, but Jeannie's looking for you. She's over there." Troy pointed to the other corner of the room.

"Hey, Jeannie. Troy said you were looking for me," Steve greeted as he came near.

"Hi, Steve. Glad you could make it to class. How's your mom? I…we've all been so worried."

"She's much better. The first few days were tough. She's recovering well from the concussion, and her leg is mending."

"I'm so glad she's all right. Do you want to sit together tonight?"

No sign of Ronnie. He figured he shouldn't be rude. "Sure." A heavy sigh escaped, as his mind and heart wondered where she might be. Was she avoiding him?

Jeannie looked his way, a slight question in her expression.

He smiled at her, not wanting to express his doubts about Ronnie being absent. Jeannie was nice enough and very good at her job, but seeing her didn't spark one bit of interest in his heart. Now, Ronnie...she made his insides go all mushy, and, if hearts could do cartwheels of joy, his would do that, too. Not that he'd ever admit that to the guys. They'd rib him for the rest of his life if they ever found that out. A man had to have standards.

Jeannie broke into his thoughts. "It must have been so hard for you to see your mom's accident happen."

"Yeah, but she's going to be OK. Her head has cleared pretty well. I think the shock of it all was the worst part for her. Did I miss much from the last class?"

"Nothing you don't already know. I can give you my notes if that would help."

"Sure. That'd be great. Thanks."

Ronnie walked in.

Their gazes met briefly, and then she rushed over to a table near the back wall.

Humph. Well, guess he'd sit with Jeannie tonight.

~*~

Ronnie had spotted Steve, contemplated turning back to run to her car, but instead she darted to a rear table with an empty chair. She didn't care who she sat next to tonight as long as it wasn't Steve. Even if she had to sit next to Troy.

Surely Steve wouldn't want to sit with the

person who sent his mom into the icy waters of the creek and caused all that pain and suffering. How would she ever stop this obsessive repeating of the scene inside her mind?

Troy leaned his shoulder into hers. "Guess we get to partner up tonight. Maybe we could practice mouth to mouth resuscitation." His right eyebrow raised up.

"Focus, Troy. You're here to learn something, remember?" She really disliked his constant attempts to impress her. Or whatever he thought he was doing.

The instructor began the class explaining how they were to now start their rotations with the ambulance teams. His warnings about the things they would see and experience made Ronnie cringe a bit. Part of the job though. If she wanted to be an EMT, she'd have to face some serious traumatic injuries. Hopefully she'd never come across someone she knew again.

Saturdays were the long class. For six hours she avoided Steve. Hiding out on breaks in the ladies room was not her most grown-up decision, but she couldn't think of a better way to keep away from him.

Near the end of the late afternoon lesson, every pager in the room went off.

All talking ceased as they listened to the dispatcher. "Major rock slide on the highway. Mutual aid needed to extract the victims of a bus, semi, and two vehicles. Be advised, tanker truck on its side and leaking." Dispatch gave the location.

"Everybody head to the scene." The instructor was brisk. "Sounds like they need all the help they can get."

8

Firefighters and rescue personnel jumped to their feet. Chairs scraped against the floor as they headed out. In the truck bay, everyone worked as a team to load gear and themselves into the necessary vehicles, even as the large doors began to rise. People rushed to put on protective clothing and equipment, not sure what would be needed, but preparing just in case.

Lights began to flash, sirens began to scream.

Adrenaline coursed through Ronnie's veins.

A rock slide. This could be bad, especially if mutual aid had to be called in.

There hadn't been any mud or rock slides for a while, and they rarely caught vehicles. But with the snow storms lately, followed by the melting from sunny days, it increased the danger of earth moving and falling.

The line of trucks headed down the ramp onto the highway. The sun had already slipped behind the surrounding hillsides shadowing the canyon. Red and blue lights circled the roadway, bouncing off the rock walls to the side of the highway. Cars sat one after the other in a solid line of red tail lights. Another bad sign.

The drivers might have difficulty allowing them through. They did their best to move over to the side or squeeze together so the emergency vehicles could pass on the shoulders.

Highway patrolmen joined the race.

A few miles ahead, a patrol car was sitting sideways preventing the cars from proceeding.

The chaotic scene came into view under the portable lights that rose up from the trucks, illuminating the mess in the canyon.

A large casino-bound bus sat at an awkward angle with the front end crushed in. Several emergency windows were opened. Rocks of every size were strewn all over; one, the size of a microwave oven, sat in the middle of the hood of the car that had been in the lead. One car had crashed into the bus and all of it blocked both lanes. A semi tanker truck that had been coming from the other direction lay on its side. Rocks had piled up next to it.

"Where do we begin?" She muttered aloud. Ronnie shivered uncontrollably not knowing if it was from the nighttime air moving in or the seriousness of the scene. She tightened up her collar.

A fire truck ahead of her rescue rig had stopped and yellow clad people, helmets in place, poured out of the vehicle. Firefighters rushed to tend to the victims. The other two departments were extricating wounded people off the bus. They had set up a triage area several yards ahead of the whole scene.

Matt pulled their vehicle into the chaos.

Ronnie jumped out and ran with the large medical bag up toward that area. Her heart lurched and she hoped no one had been killed.

The deafening noise of several Jaws of Life working at removing twisted metal dimmed the screams from pain. The heavy smell of diesel filled the air. Everyone worked together doing what they were trained to do. Dispatch called over the radio for the rock mitigation teams to get to the scene. Hazmat teams already surrounded the leaking fuel with absorbent pads. They'd have to bring in another tanker and transfer the rest of the fuel, which would be a whole other issue with the size of this slide.

Ronnie reached one victim, who had been placed on a tarp. The woman had a lot of blood on her face and one arm had an obvious compound fracture. Ronnie shivered, despite her experience. Compound fractures were the worst, the pain was unrelenting. She went to work, cleaning and bandaging the woman's head. An EMT came over to take care of the arm.

The woman moaned, but her eyes didn't open, which was a blessing, despite the seriousness of her condition.

An odd popping noise echoed nearby. Ronnie looked around, trying to discern the source of the sound. It happened again.

EMTs carried what appeared to be the last victim away from the bus. All the other personnel also walked away.

Pop. Pop. She searched again. A few small rocks were coming down. Several more rapid pops echoed in the canyon. She jumped up, her breath hitched in her throat before she found the strength to scream. "Get out of there! It's going to slide. Move!" She waved her arm, shrieking as loud as she could. "Move it! Move along! Get out!"

Crews didn't hesitate. One of their own was screaming instructions and they obeyed instantly. Ambulatory victims were hurried along by the emergency personnel.

Ronnie grabbed the tarp under her own victim, the EMT gripped the other side and they picked up the woman, taking her to the triage area, away from the wrecks. Ronnie and her unknown partner, set the tarp down, trying not to jostle their charge too much and then threw themselves over the woman, shielding her body from what was to come.

Everyone hit the road face down, some of the personnel arched over their victims, just as Ronnie and her partner had done.

Dirt, brush, rock, and boulders slid off the mountain, finishing off the bus and pushing the semi further into the ditch. The roaring that filled the air as tons of earth cascaded off the mountain caused her to cover her ears.

Movement stopped and an eerie silence filled the air. Someone coughed, breaking the thrall that held them as people warily waited for more. Dust hung over the area like a fog. And then everyone scrambled to check on each other. Names were called as people checked in with their teams.

Thankfully, enough ambulances had arrived and gurneys had been stationed next to the tarp, so Ronnie assisted loading patients to get them out of the area as the choking dust began to clear.

No one mentioned what was on all their minds.

There could be even more instability up on the mountain, and it could release just as easily as it had before.

They had to get the injured out of there.

~*~

His Ronnie had saved every single person on the scene. His Ronnie. She'd object to that, but as Steve searched his heart, he knew it to be true. She was his once-in-a-lifetime love. He tucked the information away to savor for another time, and renewed the vow in his soul to make her see she was meant for him alone.

Steve went back to check the semi's leak. The liquid had been sopped up by the excess soil from the second slide. Thankfully, nothing had ignited; the dirt had smothered any sparks. Dust still hung in the air, but visibility was much better than even a few minutes ago. And this was the most frightening thing he'd ever seen. They'd had rocks come down before, but this one took most of the hill and blocked the entire road. And therein was another big issue. All the vehicles from Steve's department were on the other side of the massive pile of boulders, trees and dirt.

The chief walked up.

Steve pointed to the mountain that had rolled down to stand between them and their trucks. "Looks like we'll have a problem getting home. This will take some time to clear."

"When county says the hillside is stable enough, we'll have to make our way over this mess to the trucks. I hope they weren't damaged."

"Ronnie warned everyone."

"I know. She'll be receiving a commendation for that."

"Looks like they've finished loading everyone. I want to talk to her." Steve walked over to where Ronnie stood talking to Jeannie.

Sirens filled the air as the ambulances took off with the victims. Others were getting on a bus that had been brought in to transport people whose injuries were minor and those without medical problems.

Only emergency personnel remained behind.

Steve's department needed to return to their jurisdiction in case other calls came in, but they had to wait for county to give them the OK.

They didn't need more rocks coming down on people.

He interrupted the two women. "What a

disaster. Good thing you figured that out." He pointed to the slide.

"I heard it as it started to come down." Ronnie's gaze darted away from him. "I…need to go help…uh, I'll see you later."

"Ronnie…"

But she got away fast.

"That has to be the worst call we've had." Jeannie turned a half circle, looking over the scene.

"Yeah, I've never seen a slide like that."

"This was my first call with such serious injuries." Her voice broke a bit.

"It never gets easy to see that."

"Have you dealt with this before?"

"Huh?" His attentions were still elsewhere. "Yeah, unfortunately. Rarely do we get that many injured at one time, though. Can't believe no one died in this."

Ronnie went out of sight.

Steve turned his attention to the mountainous pile of dirt and dust still swirling around. The road damage in some spots would require repair before cars could drive on it.

"Do you think we could get together? Maybe meet for coffee or something?" Dust marred her scrunched-up face, but sadness was evident from what she'd witnessed.

It was important to deal with the emotions of a call like this. If she felt better talking to a team mate before talking to a counselor, he had to be there. That's what being a team meant, having each other's backs, and when necessary, their attention.

"Uh, sure. We could do that." He found himself saying. He didn't want to be rude, but he'd prefer coffee with Ronnie. Still, if Jeannie needed to decompress, he'd be there for her.

"Tomorrow morning? We could meet downtown at the coffee shop." Hope entered her expression.

"OK. About 8:00?" He was glad the sadness was gone. She'd be all right after a talk with him, and maybe he'd suggest she see the counselor just to be sure.

"That sounds great." She turned to help with gathering up their gear.

Steve started walking in the direction Ronnie went, hoping to find her.

Troy caught him. "Hey, when are they going to let us get over to our trucks?"

"The engineers over there are checking the slide area. It shouldn't be long."

"I think it'd be fine if we walked over on the other side there." Troy pointed to the ditch.

"We have to have clearance, Troy. Just wait it out. Go make yourself useful."

"Fine." Troy's tone was disgruntled.

Steve had no doubt the young man would learn, or be asked to leave the department. He walked away, towards where he'd last seen Ronnie.

"Everyone, gather around over here." The chief was near the other department's truck and under the light extended above it. "We've been given the OK. Make sure we have all our gear. The front-end loader is clearing some of the debris so we can get over to our trucks. Debriefing at the station before anyone goes home. The road will be closed for a while, so we'll have to assist in calls on our side if need be."

The loud beeping of the earth mover now filled the canyon. The operator worked carefully near the overturned tanker moving the debris so they could get another truck in to transfer the load.

Steve would have to try later to talk to Ronnie.

~*~

The next morning, he got to the coffee shop a little before eight.

Jeannie already sat drinking her coffee and waved at him.

"Hi, Jeannie. I'm going to go grab a coffee. I'll be right back."

"Great." She smiled up at him.

Steve ordered up his plain black coffee, after an odd look from the barista.

The steam escaped the small hole in the plastic cap as he set it down on the table across from her. No more dirt smudges on her face like last night. He slipped his jacket off and threw it to the corner of the bench seat. The rich aroma drifted up and filled his nostrils.

"Quite a call yesterday, wasn't it? I never would have imagined a slide that bad."

"Worst one yet. Pretty much a miracle that there were no fatalities." Steve took a tentative sip so he wouldn't burn his tongue.

"The news this morning said there were a few still in critical condition. I hope they all pull through."

"Yeah, I know. I hear the road is still closed, too. It will be a mess for a while. Are you OK with it all?"

"I guess." She looked down at her hands surrounding her cup.

A distinct mocha smell drifted over to him. He never could understand messing up a good cup of coffee.

"It was so chaotic when we got there. The injuries were horrible. I got concerned if we'd get to everyone in time. Did you see that one guy's leg?" She shivered as her eyes closed briefly.

"Yeah, he's got a long recovery ahead."

"You were great out there." She leaned toward him.

He slid to the corner of the booth and stretched his leg along the bench. "I've been at this a lot longer than you. You did fine, though. No worries there. You have to kind of steel yourself against what you see and just do the job."

"I hope that gets easier. I didn't really think about it until we were done with everything." Jeannie reached back to gather her dark hair with both hands and twisted it behind her head.

"Not really easier, but more routine. You sort of go through the motions without thinking about what's really going on. Ronnie sure saved the day, though."

Jeannie leaned back. "Yeah, she did."

"We'd have all been in bad shape if she hadn't realized that next slide was coming. It could have been a lot worse."

"Uh huh. So…have you had many difficult calls?"

"Oh, yeah. Several. We rolled on an assist call with rescue after a guy on a motorcycle took a turn and the person in the car didn't see him. They hit him and he landed about fifty feet from the bike. A witness said he flew up in the air when hit. Broke both his legs. The other driver was completely oblivious that a bike had been there. The victim was a professional athlete, too."

"That's terrible. Poor guy."

"I read in the newspaper it ruined his career."

"Sad. Must have been a tough call."

"Yeah, but we've had worse, too."

"Like what?" Jeannie shifted and scooted forward again.

"Oh, man, we've had a couple really bad house fires. Then that huge fire a couple years ago in the national forest that spread into the residential areas. We get elk through windshields, then the bomb threat at the high school. That turned out to be a prank, but sure had the whole town in a panic. Parents, kids, teachers running around looking for each other..."

"Wow." Jeannie put her chin in her hand. Fascination took over her expression. "Scary stuff."

"The challenges make it more interesting. So are you off today?"

"No, my shift starts soon. I just thought it'd be nice if we could talk for a bit." She shifted in her seat. "Would you want to catch a movie with me sometime?"

"Oh, um..." She was asking him out? On a date? He hadn't seen that coming. Now what would he do? His mind scrambled, immediately going to what Ronnie would think. Jeannie seemed like a nice girl, but his heart still belonged to Ronnie. The racing thoughts made him wonder maybe if Ronnie were jealous, she'd come around. Didn't seem fair to Jeannie though. What to say? What to say? "My schedule is kind of crazy right now. Work, class, helping my mom...but maybe when things level out."

Her face no longer held the smile. She slouched a bit on the bench. Uh oh. She looked disappointed.

He didn't want to do that either, but it wouldn't be fair to her when his heart belonged to Ronnie.

"Oh, sure. I get it." Her gaze wandered around the coffee shop.

The noise level had increased with more

patrons.

"I guess I should get to work then." She stood and grabbed her cup.

"I'll probably see you later." He stood, too.

"Yeah, sure." She walked out the door.

He sat down to finish his coffee. He couldn't remember the last time he'd been asked out on a date. Come to think of it, had he ever been asked out? With his heart set on Ronnie for so many years, he may not have noticed. Would it hurt to go out with someone else? No, it'd just be weird. He only wanted to date Ronnie. No one else mattered. He had to talk to her.

They had stuff to work out.

She had done a great job of avoiding him. Did she feel guilty about his mom's accident? He'd seen everything from the hill side. There was no way to stop that car from going in the creek, even though she and Matt had tried. They simply couldn't argue with...how had Matt phrased it...*puny humans against three thousand pounds of steel.*

He had to see her. That was his priority right now. Not dating someone else.

9

"Captain, I don't want this." Ronnie hated to whine.

"Ronnie, you saved everyone on scene that night. Had you not screamed when you did for everyone to run, we'd have had countless fatalities. Why are you bucking this so strongly?"

"Sir, I don't deserve any recognition for doing my job. Everyone did their job."

"Special circumstances get noticed. You are receiving this award regardless. Ten o'clock tomorrow morning."

How ridiculous. She didn't deserve a commendation. Someone else would have figured it out. She just realized another slide was coming first. The only honor she should get was for worst decision maker ever.

In the morning, she yanked a little too hard on her hair as she pulled it up into a high ponytail. Her dress uniform shirt with badge seemed to mock her in the mirror. She hated that she'd have to stand up in front of the department to receive this bogus award.

She had made a stupid mistake that almost cost one life. At the scene of the slide, she'd simply been far enough away from the machinery noise to pick up on the rocks popping on the hill. Anyone could have heard it if they'd been there.

Ten minutes before she had to leave, she flung herself into the chair, arms hanging over each side. She closed her eyes thinking of all the victims of the first slide. But then her mind's eye switched over to another scene: Debra's car flipping down the embankment and landing in the icy water.

Tears filled Ronnie's eyes. She sat up. She was not cut out for this job. Not like her dad. Maybe she should quit. But what would she do? She's never done anything else. Well, except for that first part-time job filling ice cream cones—badly.

Her dad used to tease her that she needed to line-up with God's will, or she'd never make a good cone. What would her dad tell her now? That was easy. He'd be harping on her to buck up.

With a heavy sigh, she got her work boots. Sitting back on the couch, she laced them up, took a deep breath, and then headed out the door.

When she walked into the conference room, it was packed with almost the entire department. Great. Oh, no…a reporter, too? She groaned as the captain waved her to the front.

"And here is our hero of the hour, Ronnie Spencer!"

The room erupted in applause with all the firefighters and rescue workers jumping to their feet. Whistles pierced the air.

Ronnie was sure her face changed to three shades of magenta as the heat poured out of her collar. She tried to smile. She really did. But it just would not come up. She didn't deserve their cheers. She'd practically killed Mrs. McNeal, with a massive error in judgment. She walked to the front, stood next to the captain, and dared a glance up from her feet.

Steve was right up front clapping wildly.

The captain spoke, but she heard nothing. How could they stand there cheering for her after Mrs. McNeal's disaster? She wished for a hole to open and swallow her up.

"So, Ronnie, we want to acknowledge that you saved all of us from serious injury and quite possibly death. We present you with this commendation, along with our heartfelt thanks." He extended a framed certificate and shook her hand.

She smiled back at him, feeling like a fraud. "Thank you sir." Taking the frame, she stepped back, wanting to run from the room.

Everyone came forward to congratulate her.

She'd never shaken so many hands.

Most of them gave her a huge pat on the back, too. Her face was hot, sweat dripped between her shoulder blades, and she was sure redness was building on her cheeks.

Steve hung back.

She was certain he wouldn't take part in

this sham after what she did to his mother, despite his enthusiastic clapping earlier. He was polite enough to not condemn her in front of the others. Her father had often talked about taking a problem to the source in private, and she was sure Steve would do the same.

Steve moved up after the last person stepped away.

She couldn't look at him.

"Hey, you. Congrats. I'm sure glad you heard that slide coming." He reached out to give her a hug.

She stepped back fast. "Well, thanks, but you know I don't deserve this." She had to get out of there. Her legs twitched with the need to run. "Excuse me…" she pushed her way around him and rushed from the room. Once in her truck, the tears flowed. She threw the commendation on the passenger side floor face down. She couldn't bear to look at the thing.

10

Someone knocked on the door of her apartment.

Ronnie looked at the clock. Noon. She put her eye to the peep hole, saw Steve, and groaned. Leaning her head against the door, she had no idea what she would say to him. She had to face this now.

He knocked again.

She took a deep breath and opened the door. "Hi."

"Hi, Ronnie. I was worried about you. Can I come in?"

"Uh, sure."

Concern etched deep lines in his forehead.

"I'm just watching the news. They covered the rock slide." She grabbed the remote and turned the television off. "Have a seat."

He sat on the couch.

She sat on the chair.

"Sounds like they're still trying to clear the road."

"They showed a helicopter view. Still quite a mess." She bit her lower lip, pulled up the courage to ask a nagging question, but one she didn't want to talk about. "Is your mom OK?"

"Oh, yeah, she's fine. Still on crutches, but she's getting around fine."

Ronnie fought a sigh. "I heard you had taken time off to help her. I worried she'd gotten worse."

"No, I'm just the only one around able to help her. I had the time, so I figured why not. The slide was my first call back. Nothing like jumping back in the fire," he said with a chuckle.

Ronnie couldn't look at him. She took in a deep breath, desperately seeking the nerve to say what she had to say.

"Ronnie—"

She cut his words off. "Steve, I need to say something." She went to the window. "I'm so sorry for causing your mom's injuries. I just can't believe I did something so stupid-"

"What?" his loud tone made the shock more evident. "Ronnie...you're not at fault."

She turned to face him. "Yes I am. If I hadn't tried to put that log under the front end, the car wouldn't have gone over. Don't you see? I did that to her." She returned to looking out the window.

"I saw from the truck as we made our way to the scene. That car was teetering over, no matter what you think or saw. I talked to Matt. He says the same. The center of gravity meant nothing would've stopped it except a winch, and the truck didn't get there in time for that. You had to try something. I would've, too. And it would've been just as fruitless. Matt said he could feel it slipping out of his grasp. You had a good idea; it just didn't work. And Mom's going to be OK, so just being there saved her, she wasn't in the car long enough to get hypothermia, or die of shock or anything else that could've killed her if she'd been down there any longer."

~*~

He had to find a way to get through to her. He should have come sooner. He felt like such an idiot. He reached out a hand to touch her shoulder, turning her gently toward him. "Ronnie…"

Tears ran down her face. She wouldn't look up at him. Her shoulders were stiff and tight. Her breath caught, a sob escaped and her head fell into his chest.

He held her tight. "Come here." He walked her over to the couch. They sat as one, and he continued to hold her close to him. As she wept, he worked at forming the right words. "Listen. We understand how the accident happened. We're thankful you and Matt were there to help her. You had a challenging situation to deal with. You were able to get to her right away. That made a huge difference."

She sat up abruptly. "Had I not forced the car over the edge, she wouldn't even have a broken leg." Her words had a sharp enough edge to cut.

"Ronnie, we're in an unpredictable

business. We just have to do the best we can with whatever situation comes."

"I feel so bad, Steve. I could have killed your mom."

"She's going to be fine."

She brought her knees up to her chest and held her legs. "I keep reliving the whole thing in my head. I wish I'd have done things different."

"We all have calls like that sooner or later, Ronnie. We can only learn from them. We have to learn from them."

Her head rested against her knees. "I know. I just wish it hadn't been your mom. That may sound terrible. I mean, I wouldn't wish this on anyone, but…well…with our past…I just feel so awful."

Steve didn't know how to respond. Did that mean she still cared? She hadn't been acting as if she had any feelings for him anymore. His heart beat harder, a mad pulse that seemed to swish so loud she should be able to hear it. He sat there, staring at her coffee table and waited.

He thought of his own guilt with her dad. He totally understood where she was coming from, but his mom survived. He didn't think his empathy would be well received by her. The subject always proved to be touchy.

"Now you really think I'm terrible, don't you?" She sniffed and looked up at him.

"No I don't. I can understand that. I wish it hadn't been mom, too. But it was." He shrugged his shoulders feeling the tension that had built up in his neck muscles. He took the chance. "I've always wished it hadn't been your dad, either. I know how easy it is to stay in the trap of guilt and sadness. I did for a long time after we lost your dad, but you have to reach a point of letting it go when it can't be changed anyway. It's a real struggle. I get that."

"Do you?"

"Yes, I do, Ronnie. Seems to me we've both had the same test."

"I've never done well on tests."

"We'll get through all of this. Mom will heal up. You need to move on now. Stop beating yourself up."

"I'm trying. I'm not very good at it." The start of a smile developed on her lips. "I find it much easier to beat myself up."

Steve laughed. "I have noticed that about you."

She elbowed him.

He debated on taking a chance to ask, but knew what her answer would be. He stalled, on purpose, since the anticipation of a "yes" seemed better than the "no" he knew he'd probably receive.

He took a deep breath in the awkward silence. "The department Christmas party is coming up at the beginning of December. Do you want to go with me?"

She lowered her legs and shifted away from him.

Not a good sign.

"Steve…" her hand went under her hair as she rubbed the back of her neck. "There's all kinds of wrong in that question."

"Come on, Ronnie. We've been having fun in class. Come to the party with me. It's just a get together. You know most of the department anyway."

"Steve, I don't want to date you. We're coworkers and friends. That's it. Take Jeannie. She'd love to go with you."

Jeannie? Where'd that come from? "Ronnie, I don't want to go with anyone else. I want to be with you. I've enjoyed our time together. Haven't you? It seems as if we've been getting along great."

"As friends," she emphasized. "This isn't dating. This is being in the same class."

"Well, this is just a party. Come with me. Have some fun."

"No. I won't date you, and I don't celebrate Christmas. Not anymore."

"Why not? It's the most special time of year. It's the birthday of Christ."

Her back went rigid. "All those decorations, trees, shopping for things no one wants anyway…there's no point to it."

"The ornaments are memories on branches. The lights remind me of the Light He brought into the world. The gifts, well, the gifts are an example of what God gifted us with. The gift of our Savior, and everlasting life."

"I know where you're coming from, Steve.

But I just can't do it anymore. My dad felt the same way you do. He always made it so special. He did crazy things every Christmas like wearing his Santa hat the whole month of December. He even wore it to work. He lit up the house so much you could land planes on our street." Her eyes took on a distant gaze. "He hung small wreaths on our bedroom doors with a little box dangling from them with small gifts inside for Adam and me. Dad put a new gift in them every day. We'd be so excited every morning to see what the new trinket would be. He made it so special." She sighed and bit her lip. "With him gone, it's just too painful to remember. It just makes me mad when Christmas comes. I just don't care anymore." Her lower lids pooled up with tears.

Steve slid closer and wrapped his hand around her tightly clenched hands. "What can I do to help you through this?"

"Oh, Steve. Nothing." She pulled her hands away. "I just have to get through the holiday. I won't acknowledge it. It isn't fair that he's gone. I miss him so much." She reached for a few tissues to dry her eyes and blow her nose.

Steve had no words to help. There had to be some way he could bring comfort to her. A plan began to take shape in his mind.

11

Steve walked into the department Christmas party in full swing.

A fully decorated tree sat on the opposite wall from the door. Many of the spouses were there with coworkers.

He loved this annual get together, but wished for Ronnie to be by his side.

Music blared and laughter filled the room. He grabbed a bottle of water off the beverage table and joined a group of guys off to the side who were giving Troy a hard time. The rookie dished it right back—only with a bad attitude.

Steve turned around to find a group without Troy in it. He didn't want the frustration tonight.

Jeannie touched his arm. "Hi, Steve. I wondered if you would come. How are you?"

"Oh, hi, Jeannie. I'm good. Fun party," he said over the noise in the room.

"Yeah, it is."

People were on the dance floor. It was getting crazy out there as they laughed and moved to the music.

"Do you dance?"

"Huh," Steve turned back to Jeannie. "Me?

No. Not me. I don't dance."

"Oh."

Disappointment covered on her face.

No, dancing was not something he would do, especially watching the guys out there flailing around. Not happening.

"Would you like to go sit down and talk?" Her look was hopeful.

"Uh, sure." Steve pointed to an open table off to the side. "It might be quieter over there."

They sat and looked over the crowd.

Steve didn't know what to talk about with her. She wanted more than he could give and he didn't want her to get an idea that he'd changed his mind.

"Looks like Troy's annoying the guys again." Jeannie pointed.

The man's animated movements were evident that he was bragging on himself. Soon he stood alone drinking his glass of soda, one hand in a pocket.

"He's not making friends."

"I know. He bugs everyone. It's too bad." She grimaced.

"I think he could be a good firefighter if he'd calm down some. Maybe he'll get it by watching the others on the job. Like Ronnie. She's great at her job. She sure saved our necks at the rock slide."

"Yeah, I suppose."

"You suppose? If she hadn't been paying attention, who knows what might have happened to all of us? She was really in tune with that situation. I'm still amazed we weren't all killed."

Jeannie leaned back, slouching in her chair. She wasn't listening any more. Her gaze went to the crowd at the food table.

"All I'm saying is I'm glad she warned everyone." His tone was awkward, even he could hear it.

"But doesn't it bother you what she did at your mom's accident?"

"No!" His voice turned sharp. What was she implying? "Can you think of a better option if you'd been in her shoes?"

"Well, no, but the car did go over when she tried to put that log under there."

"The car was already going over, no matter what. She tried to stop it. We could see from the top of the road it was no use. Mom went over the edge because of the law of gravity, not because of anything Ronnie did or didn't do. It was a tough situation they faced." Steve squared his shoulders. His forehead pinched at her comments and attitude. Did others blame Ronnie, too?

"I'm not implying anything, just…well, curious how you felt about that."

"Accidents happen. Matt said the car would have gone regardless. He could barely hang onto it. His exact quote was, 'Two puny humans had no chance against three thousand pounds of steel.' Ronnie still managed to prevent a huge tragedy at the rock slide. The job is up and down all the time. Every call is different."

"True."

The captain walked over to their table. "Hey, how are you two doing? Merry Christmas."

Steve stood and shook his hand. "Merry Christmas. Join us?"

"Sure. Thanks."

Thankful for getting out of that conversation, he turned his attention to the captain. "We were just talking about the slide."

"What a disaster! Sure could have been worse if…"

Jeannie's hands hit the table hard as she pushed back her chair. "Excuse me." She headed to the food table.

Humph, weird. Even the captain looked puzzled, so Steve knew it wasn't just him wondering.

The captain looked after her. "Was it something I said?"

Steve shrugged.

12

Time for his plan. A convoluted plan, but Steve was determined. If Christmas had become too difficult for Ronnie without her dad making it special, he would restart the tradition. A light snow started, putting him in an even better mood to work on creating something spectacular for her.

"It's a brilliant idea, Steve." Mrs. Spencer was ecstatic.

"It will shake her out of her 'bah, humbug' mood, too." Adam was just as approving.

"Adam!" Mrs. Spencer glared at her son.

"It's true, Mom," Adam protested. "Since Dad died, Ronnie doesn't even want to celebrate."

"Well, when she sees what Steve will do, and we assure her we love her dearly, maybe this will stop some of the heartache," Mrs. Spencer nodded to Steve. "We'll take Ronnie to lunch so you should have plenty of time."

Later, as he hauled the boxes and bags of decorations up three flights of stairs, which proved difficult since he still had a slight limp, Steve wondered if he was crazy. And then, wrestling the large, bulky box holding the artificial tree, he decided he'd do whatever he needed for the woman he loved. The last trip down to the car would retrieve the most important box, a long one from the florist.

It was weird to be in her place without her, but this would be totally worth it.

Steve tuned the radio for background Christmas music to help his project along, and then he began to set up the tree. The new decorations he bought included a fire truck and ambulance ornaments. He strung lights, laid down a tree skirt, added the ornaments, and, finally, he reached up and attached the lighted star, held by an angel.

He placed a small Nativity on her coffee table, tossed a soft, cozy Christmas blanket and pillow on a chair, added a small basket with hot chocolate, a mug, and a snack on the end table and stepped back to look at his creation. It looked good.

Finding a large vase, he opened the florist box and pulled out the multi-colored roses. How did one arrange these things? Dropping them all into the vase, he haphazardly stabbed the small white flowers in and around the roses. He pulled out the card he'd created from the box and leaned it against the vase. Taking a moment, Steve admired his work. "Well, God, I've done my best. Please let her like it." He didn't want to acknowledge that his future children would depend on their mother loving Christmas...who was he kidding? He wanted Ronnie. For now and always. He acknowledged that and his future children freely.

Gathering up the empty boxes and bags, he locked her door and hauled the stuff back out to his car. "God, don't let this backfire on me."

~*~

Ronnie loved going to lunch with her mom. Having Adam join them added to the familial warm fuzzies. She couldn't remember the last time the three of them had gone out to lunch together. But then the memory struck her. The last time all three of them sat in a restaurant, they had to decide what to do with Dad's service. She breathed in a heavy burden.

All the Christmas music and decorations drove her nuts. Everywhere she went, Christmas. Cheery good will to all. Except her. Nothing about it made her feel cheery. It would be a relief to get back to her apartment away from all of that.

Unlocking the door, she walked into a department store window display. Her purse and keys fell to the floor. "What in the world?" Walking slowly into the living area, she couldn't believe her eyes. A tree sat in front of the patio door lit with a gazillion colored lights. Ornaments of every color also filled in the branches. A fire truck ornament hung prominently in the center front, with an ambulance next to it. She lifted it with a shaking hand. As she turned, she noticed the pine garland that adorned the archway leading to the bedroom. On the side table sat a huge bouquet of multicolored roses. The coffee table, the end table…it all looked so homey, so comfortable…so Christmas.

She stood in the center of the room, turned in a slow circle, and tried to take it all in. A pool of tears formed in her eyes blurring the sight. She walked over to read the card leaning against the vase.

"I wanted to make Christmas special this year by decorating for you. The flowers are to tell you how I feel about you: a pink rose to symbolize your grace and elegance so you know how much I admire you and the work you do. A yellow one to say how much I appreciate our friendship and it brings me joy. A white rose for the newness of our hoped-for relationship. An orange one to express my excitement and passion for you. The red rose to say how much I still love you. And last, but not least, the lavender one to tell you I am enchanted with you. You captured my heart long ago. Love, Steve."

She stared in disbelief and her hands dropped to her side. She fell back onto the couch and tears spilled over and ran down her cheeks. Ronnie raised the card once more, looked at the words, and flung it like a Frisbee across the room. It stuck dead center in the decorated tree on the far side of the room, spinning the fire truck ornament violently.

13

Ronnie hadn't called. She had to be home.

Returning the key to Mrs. Spencer, Steve shared the excitement of the plan.

"I'm pretty sure she went straight home from lunch."

Sitting in his jeep a block away, he stared at his cell phone willing it to ring. Maybe he should go over. No, maybe he should wait.

Did she love it?

He was certain he'd done a good job, for a guy. She had to have seen his card. He worked hard on it last night, wanting the words to be just right. Looking it up on line to find the meanings of the different colors for roses helped him compose it. He had no idea before that rose colors meant something.

Adjusting the radio volume again, he tapped on the steering wheel to the beat of the music. "Lord, I just want her to love Christmas again. OK, and maybe love me, too."

The wait tore at his insides. He had to know. He shifted the jeep into gear, drove over to her place, and parked.

Her truck sat in the parking lot, so she was home.

His cell phone didn't show any missed calls.

Christmas lights shone through the sheers covering the patio doors.

Didn't she like it?

He headed up to the door and knocked. It took forever for her to answer.

"Ronnie?" He waited with his hands in his pockets.

When she opened the door, redness puffed in her eyes and nose.

Uh oh, crying. He stood there like a lump wondering if they were good tears or bad tears, suddenly feeling seven years old. Anxiety filled his heart. "Hi," he dared utter the word.

She stepped aside. "Come on in." The words seemed to come through gritted teeth as her head turned away.

Visions of her jumping into his arms and kissing him all over his face filled his mind, the excitement bursting from her. Nope. This was not at all the response he imagined. *Uh-oh.*

She sat hard onto the couch.

He stood there, hands in his pockets, rocking back and forth. Looking over at the tree, he noticed his card stuck oddly in the branches, barely hanging onto the perch. He bit his lip.

Tears began to stream down her beautiful face.

He scratched his head then warily sat next to her. Not too close for fear of where this reaction would go. What should he say? "I...take it...I blew it." His fingers worked against each other. He stilled them, embarrassed to think he was actually wringing his hands.

She grabbed a tissue from the box on the side table and blew her nose. "What were you thinking, Steve? You know how I feel about Christmas."

"I thought if I started a new tradition it might help you enjoy it again."

"What gave you the right to decide that for me?" Her voice rose as anger filled her tone. "How can I enjoy something that reminds me of not having my father around anymore? This…" she stood and swung her hand around at the décor he worked so hard on. "…doesn't work. Dad didn't do it."

"I don't think he would want you to not celebrate Christmas ever again. He had faith. He loved you. He would want you to go on."

"How dare you think you know what he would want?"

He winced. Everything in him wanted to run out of the apartment to avoid believing he'd blown it this badly.

As if reading his mind, she said, "You need to leave, Steve. Right now. I can't talk to you about this." She started walking toward the door. "You can't possibly understand."

"Ronnie, I want to understand. I want to help. I wanted you to know how much I love you and care about you."

"Listen, I get what you meant to do.

Really, I do." Her voice was brittle and her jaw twitched. "I know you meant well, but it's just too hard. Every time I look at a tree, the memories flood back of my dad running around the house in his Santa hat, playing the new games with us. It just hurts so bad." The tears began again. "I miss him so much."

"But...aren't they good memories?" *Oops. That look. Apparently, that wasn't the right thing to say either.* Steve didn't know what to do. He usually chose wrong when it came to women crying, which he learned growing up with sisters. Tentatively, he reached out to touch her arm.

She gulped, a sob slipped out, and then she melted into his arms, her head against his chest.

He kept his mouth shut and just held her as she cried. How he wanted to hold her forever. He brushed her hair behind her ear then held her cheek in the palm of his hand. Dare he speak? "You have incredible memories of a great man and an especially great father. That is a huge blessing." Dampness reached his skin through his shirt.

The words of 2 Corinthians 1:3-4 came into his head. *Praise be to the God and Father of our Lord Jesus Christ, the Father of compassion and the God of all comfort, who comforts us in all our troubles, so that we can comfort those in any trouble with the comfort we ourselves receive from God.*

She sniffed.

"You have a Father in heaven who loves

you just as much."

"I just don't understand why God took him away." She pushed away.

Their eyes met, hers searching his for answers.

"I don't know why it happened, Ronnie, but God didn't do it. The fire and smoke caused your dad's death. Not God. We can't confuse God with life. Stuff happens because of events. Consequences."

"He still could have saved him. *You* could have saved him."

He suddenly understood why people claimed their hearts stopped when faced with shock. He couldn't move or speak. His helplessness rose to the surface, chewing him up from the inside out. Would he ever come to terms with his inability to do anything to save the man?

She really did blame him. Deep down. The pain in her eyes spoke volumes.

How would he ever reach past that pain to have her love him again? And more importantly, forgive him. "Ronnie…I'm sorry. I couldn't do anything. You know policy. I tried to go after them, but they ordered me back."

"But couldn't you have defied the order to save my dad?"

"I didn't know what else to do. I hadn't had enough training at that point." He wanted her to understand. "He took off his mask to save John. If I'd gone in…he couldn't save both of us. Others would have had to risk their lives to go in after all three of us."

"I didn't mean to say that."

Pain splintered his own heart. She blamed him. All these years, she'd blamed him. "I wanted to go in. I really did. If I could have changed it, I would have." His voice was husky with the shards of grief.

"I do get that. I do. I just wish he could have been saved."

"Yeah, me, too." He took her hand. "We can never understand why these bad things happen. We have to trust God. God can give you the strength to get through it. It's hard to lose someone you love, but God gained him. Your dad knew Jesus. You'll see him again. God wants you to find peace in that. God is your true Father. It may not feel like it, but He knows what's best. He loves you."

"It's just so hard to comprehend, Steve. Do you know what I'm saying? I really like you, I do. Deep down I love what you did here. I love how you wanted to make up for what my dad used to do. And it's beautiful. The flowers and the card..." Ronnie stepped away and looked around the room. "I'm trying so hard to accept losing Dad. To understand God and why He allowed it. I don't like where I've been with God. I need to heal. I need a lot of help. You were the only one around when he died, and you're the only one around now who has any understanding of what I'm going through. It's too hard to talk to Mom about. I guess what I'm saying Steve, is...I need you to help me."

He had to proceed slowly, but he couldn't hide his feelings. Somehow she had to know the depth of his love for her and how he wanted years to let it grow. "You know I'm here for you. For whatever and however much you want or need. Ronnie, I love you. Very much. I have for so long. I want to help you find peace, but mostly...I just want to be with you."

That beautiful, albeit trembling, smile finally returned.

He longed to hear the words back from her.

She took his hand and led him to the couch again.

14

Saturday mornings were usually reserved for training exercises for the fire department personnel. Steve enjoyed the maneuvers, and after such a special time with Ronnie, he felt lighter, happier, more motivated. Today they were doing mock car accidents.

The sun turned the snow from overnight into a slushy mix on the pavement, rapidly turning to puddles. The temps were just right with all the gear they wore.

The training instructor asked for victim volunteers. Troy offered up his hand. A few others were chosen and the crew set up the drill. The lot behind the department had enough room to create the scenes they needed. Wrecked cars and trucks lined one side. Two of them had been moved out in the center. The victims had fake blood on them in various places and crawled through missing windows to take their positions.

As the training proceeded, Steve ended up working on the car with Troy.

The man was doing a terrible job of overacting. His over-the-top groans and hollering were unrealistic and distracting.

Steve stuck his head in the window a bit.

"Troy, you're supposed to be in shock. Shock victims don't holler. It's about the rescuers training. You're not up for an acting award."

"Hey, get over it. You're supposed to save me."

Troy's snicker irritated Steve. Hotshots had no place in this profession. Time to teach the arrogance lesson, one of long-standing in the fire department. Everyone had had enough of Troy's strutting, and he'd either learn the lesson, or be kicked off the team.

Steve pulled Kyle Hocke aside. "You want to help me humble Troy?"

"Oh yeah. Definitely." Kyle laughed.

Steve gave the signal to the captain of what needed to be done.

The firefighters doing the rescue went about their job. Steve set the Jaws of Life into the door frame and began pulling the metal apart.

Troy had been flinging insults.

The noise the device made covered whatever he was saying.

Kyle and Jeannie positioned the Stokes basket next to the car. They got their victim out of the car and into the basket to simulate a rescue where they had to hoist the vic up an incline.

Troy continued his ranting.

Steve had the straps in his hand. "We are going to strap you in for your protection now sir."

"Ha! Love it. You can call me sir, anytime." Troy wouldn't give up.

Steve fought the craving to punch him in

the hope that it would knock him out and shut him up, but decided that wouldn't be much of a professional reaction. Even if it was just a drill. He proceeded with the crisscrossing of the straps over Troy through the sides of the basket.

"Hey, kind of overdoing those straps, aren't ya? Idiot. You don't need that many. Ha, even I know that."

"Oh, I think we do..." Steve pulled the last one tighter than he really needed.

Troy let out a hard grunt.

"Good job, Steve. Now, men, take the victim over to safety." The captain grinned through the order.

Four of them picked up the Stokes, carried Troy over to the corner of the building, and stood it on end.

"Hey! What are you doing?"

But they all walked away.

Steve slapped his colleagues on the back. "Looks like it's time for break. Let's go get some coffee."

"Hey. Hey! You can't leave me here."

"Oh, you're right, Troy. You might fall. We can't have that. Guys, safety first." Steve held his finger in the air to emphasize his point. Then he grabbed the clip for the hose dryer that hung from the top of the tower. The rest of the firefighters maneuvered the ropes, and the Stokes rose up in the air just off the ground enough to hang free with the help of the pulleys above.

The firefighters walked past the elevated

man, waving as they headed into the building. One of the guys gave the Stokes a spin. Steve had strapped him in so well that he hadn't slipped an inch.

Loud protests from Troy followed them inside.

15

Ronnie arrived at Kelly Hocke's around nine in the morning. Kelly had been so excited when Ronnie had asked about a Bible study.

Ronnie couldn't take credit, it was Steve's suggestion. He'd been gentle, but he'd been firm that she needed to start learning more about God than she remembered from Sunday school. She had to do something to find some peace. *It will eat you alive otherwise.* His words echoed in her heart.

Little Stephanie swung the door open with her pig tails bouncing.

"Stephanie, what have I told you about answering the door?" Kelly admonished her daughter.

"Sorry, momma." The girl hung her head. "But I knew it'd be Miss Ronnie. You said she was coming."

"But you always have to make sure before you open the door."

"OK."

Ronnie caught the scent of the real Christmas tree that sat decorated in the corner of the living room. A heavy sigh escaped her. She had to try harder.

Kelly reached out and hugged Ronnie.

"Hi. Sorry. Come on in."

"Oh, that's fine, no problem." She walked in and knelt to hug four-year-old Stephanie. "How are you, sweetheart?"

"I'm good. Want to see my dolls?"

Ronnie stood and laughed.

Kelly placed a hand on the girl's shoulder. "Honey, Ronnie's here to spend time with me. Remember what I said? You need to go play while we talk, OK?"

Stephanie's hopeful eyes searched hers. "OK. Maybe before you go home you can come see my dollies."

"I will for sure."

The girl turned and skipped off to the steps heading up to her room.

Ronnie shook out of her coat. "She's so adorable. How are you today?" She removed her boots, too.

Kelly took her coat and hung it in the closet. "I'm good. She keeps me hopping in the mornings. Want some coffee?"

"Yes, please. That'd be great."

They headed toward the kitchen.

Kelly filled two large ceramic mugs and set them on the table. "You need any cream or sugar?"

"No, black is fine." Ronnie couldn't miss the stack of Bibles and study books. Part of her wanted to groan, but that was why she was here. She wanted to do this. No, she needed to do this. She had to find some peace for her life.

"So, where would you like to start?" Kelly asked as she reached for one of the Bibles.

"You don't waste any time." Ronnie leaned back in the chair and ran her fingers through her hair. "I don't know, Kelly. You know my struggle. I just can't find any peace about losing my dad. I don't understand. Steve wants so badly to get back together, but I just don't want to risk losing him like we lost dad. I don't think there's any hope for me getting over this."

"Sure there is. But you have to open yourself up to letting God heal your hurts. If you're willing, He'll help."

"I do know that. I just…I've been so…"

"Mad at God about it?"

Ronnie knew the tears were ready to work their way to the surface. Those words spoken out loud for the first time tipped the levee that held the tears. She had never dared to verbalize her anger toward God.

Kelly grabbed the tissue box from the counter and set it in front of Ronnie.

Dabbing at her eyes, Ronnie let the small grin creep up her face. "I'm such a sap! I get so tired of crying, yet it keeps happening."

"I know it's been hard. Your dad was far too young to go." She opened one of the Bibles and flipped through the pages. "Do you remember in the Old Testament all the times David struggled with all the bad things that kept happening to him?"

"Not really. It's been so long since I've

even thought about the Bible. We read together as a family, but with Dad gone, well…I just didn't care anymore."

"David had a lot of enemies. He had a lot of people who just wanted to destroy him. There were plenty of times he brought on a lot of it, but regardless of his grief, his struggle, his failings, the attacks against him, he always knew that he could depend on God."

"But why does God let this stuff happen?"

"I'm not sure anyone can answer that, Ronnie. But we can trust that He will get us through it all. Have you ever asked God to help you through this grief?"

Ronnie felt the heat rise in her cheeks. She bit her lower lip, met Kelly's eyes and said quietly, "I've been too mad at Him." More tears cascaded down her face. She'd have this tissue box emptied in no time. Drying her eyes, she realized a small hand rested on her knee. She looked down to see Stephanie's concerned little gaze staring up at her.

"Why are you sad, Miss Ronnie?"

"Oh, honey," Ronnie reached down to pick up the child. "Sometimes I just need to cry."

"I feel like that sometimes. You can hold my doll if you want." Stephanie handed a blonde, curly-haired doll to Ronnie. "She helps me when I'm sad."

"Thank you, Steph. I'm certain she will help me feel better, too." Ronnie did her best to smile and hugged the girl.

"OK. Go play in your room while we talk some more." Kelly stood, took the girl from Ronnie's lap, and set her on the floor.

"All right, mommy. But don't make her cry anymore."

Both women laughed.

"Let's just look at a few passages today."

Kelly passed a Bible across the table.

Ronnie flipped through the worn pages, remembering a time when reading this book had been a daily habit for her. But how long had it been? She didn't even know where she'd put her Bible.

"I want to read one verse in particular to you." Kelly flipped to the book of Isaiah.

Ronnie could see the Bible's page heading. That book had always been a challenge for Ronnie to understand.

"In chapter forty-one it says, 'Do not fear, for I am with you; do not anxiously look about you, for I am your God. I will strengthen you, surely I will help you, surely I will uphold you with My righteous right hand.'" Kelly looked up. "He's there for you, if you ask.

"God wants to help us get through things, but if you continue to hold onto your grief it becomes an obstacle for you to trust Him to help you deal. It's time to reroute your life, Ronnie. If you can work toward drawing closer to Jesus, He's waiting to help you move forward. The key is to admit you need His help, cry out for His help, and be humble enough to learn from Him."

They continued to read and discuss these truths for quite a while.

Stephanie came out again. "Momma, I'm hungry."

"I need to get going anyway." Ronnie said as she rose from the chair.

"You could stay and have a sandwich with us."

"No, thanks. Maybe next time." Ronnie reached out and hugged Kelly, then bent to hug Stephanie. "You need to show me your dolls before I go." She handed the blonde doll back to the girl.

"OK. Come on." The little girl skipped off to the stairs.

~*~

Ronnie navigated the curves in the road coming down off the mountain the Hockes lived on, smiling at the tour she had of Stephanie's dolls. Then her thoughts went to what Kelly had said about how God must have felt sending His own Son to die. A shiver ran through her. She couldn't deal with her dad's death, how God could handle what His Son had to endure was beyond comprehension.

What would her dad think of how she's been holding back on life?

He'd probably be having a long talk with her about it if he could. He always lived for the moment. Saw joy in whatever came his way. How did he do that? He was such a great man.

She choked up on how she missed him.

"OK, God." She spoke toward the windshield looking up at the sky. "I'll try. I'm not making any promises, but I'll try. But you've got to help me." Ronnie pulled into the parking lot of the grocery store. She needed milk. She beeped the auto lock and headed toward the doors.

Mrs. McNeal was coming out of the store on one of those drivable chairs.

Oh, my gosh, she can't even walk on her own. Seeing the woman for the first time after what she'd done to her...oh, no, eye contact, nowhere to hide now.

"Ronnie, hi. Oh, my goodness, I'm so glad to see you." The woman waved and attempted to get the scooter chair to go faster, which it refused to do.

"Hi, Mrs. McNeal. I'm surprised to see you out and about. How are you?"

The woman steered the chair to the side out of everyone's way. "I'm fine. Embarrassed to be in this thing, but I promised Steve. I've been going stir crazy in the house. How are you doing?"

"Oh, I'm...fine, I guess."

"You don't sound very sure."

"Well, I...I've been meaning to call and check on you. I wanted to apologize..." Ronnie couldn't look at her and hung her head. Hands in her pockets, she rocked back and forth, toe to heel. "I'm so sorry for what I did to you."

"Ronnie, it's not your fault. I never should have gone out that day. The roads were so bad, but I've been driving in snow all my life. I just didn't expect the ice. Steve sure gave me a chewing out for that. That boy forgets he's the son, not the parent." She laughed.

"I never should have tried to stick that log under there. I'm responsible for ruining your favorite car and for your injuries. I'm so sorry." Ronnie could barely see through the tears welling up in her eyes.

"Now you listen to me, young lady." The sternness of her voice caught Ronnie by surprise. "There is no way you could have known that idea wouldn't work. I shouldn't have gotten myself into that predicament. You did the best you could with me sitting there all whiney and crying for help. What happened, happened. They're called accidents for a reason. And it's been time for a new car anyway."

"Oh, Mrs. McNeal. I just wish I'd have figured something else out and spared you from all this."

"I know, sweetie, but it was an accident. No one had control that day. I'm just very thankful you were there with me. Your daddy would be so proud of you."

"I think my daddy would have chewed on me for such a dumb idea."

"Ha. I bet Frank would have done the same thing. Knowing your dad, he probably would have tried to push up the front bumper all

Superman style and put it back on the road."

Ronnie chuckled at the picture of that in her mind. Red cape and all. The blue tights…not so much. "You might be right about that. Dad was a fixer."

Mrs. McNeal reached out and took Ronnie's hand. "Seriously now, honey. I don't want you worrying about this. My leg is healing fine, a car can be replaced, and I still love you as much as always."

Ronnie sniffed. She admired this woman so much. "You know how much I love you, as well."

"I do. Thank you for being there. I mean that. It really did help to see your face that day."

"Is there anything I can do for you? Can I help you to the car?"

"Sure. Maybe you could return their handy-dandy cart thing for me."

"You bet." Ronnie walked alongside her and gave her a hand getting in the car. She loaded her bag into the back seat.

When the rental car started, Debra opened the window. "Thanks for your help. Why don't you stop by some time so we can visit like old times?"

"I'll do that. Take care now. Oh, and…drive safe!" Ronnie actually chuckled.

Debra threw her head back and laughed. "I think I will. See you soon, Ronnie."

16

Ronnie was practically skipping as she got ready for the day. She hadn't been this light-hearted in a long time and it felt good.

Steve would pick her up in half an hour to spend the day in the mountains.

When she accepted his invitation, she didn't know who was more surprised. She chuckled again remembering the shocked expression on Steve's face.

He had stammered his response; he was so startled. It was good to keep him on his toes.

Skates. Where did she put her skates? She didn't remember the last time she'd gone ice skating. Determination filled her steps, but most important, the pain seemed less in her heart.

Kelly's words rang through her mind as she searched the bottom of her closet. Her fears of loss, her insecurities, her lack of trust in God. It was time to change. Finally speaking to Debra healed so much of her pain. She never should have waited so long. "There they are!" She pulled the laces and the skates rose through the pile of shoes. Setting them by the door, she did a last minute check for the things she'd need for the day.

A knock sounded.

She jumped to the door. "Hi."

"Hi, yourself." Steve's smile lit his whole face.

"Come on in. Just getting my gloves."

"Hope you're ready for an adventure in the mountains today."

"I am. This was a great idea. I need a mountain fix."

"I have the whole day planned. Thought you might like to do some shopping in Breckenridge."

She stopped abruptly. "Wait. A guy willing to go shopping?" She had to tease.

"If you'd rather not…" Steve's eyebrows raised.

"No, no…I'm good with that."

They both laughed and headed out the door.

The sky was beautifully clear, perfect for heading up to the high country. A blue sky in Colorado seemed bluer than in most other places.

After she buckled up, she reached down for her camera. "In case there's wildlife near the road. I want pictures."

"Odds are good going past Georgetown. The rams are usually around." Steve turned the vehicle to head for I-70. "Mom said she saw you at the store."

"Yeah, we crossed paths in the parking lot. It was good to see her. Your mother is the most gracious woman."

"I told you she wasn't mad at you."

"I know. I should have remembered how kind she is. It helped so much to talk to her about the accident."

They sped by the landscape.

This was what she needed. Peace crept through her being. The mountains always did that for her. She thought back to her time with Steve before her dad died. They were good together. They'd always had fun. He was such a good friend. Maybe it was time to get that back.

She looked over at him.

He smiled at her.

Man, she loved that smile. He could melt the snow off the mountain.

Arriving in Breckenridge, he managed to find an open parking spot along the main street. The shops were festively decorated along with the lamp posts lining the road. A German shepherd with reindeer antlers on its head walked ahead of its owner. There were a lot of shoppers and skiers walking around. Winter tourism was in full swing.

"Oh, I have to go into that shop." She pointed to the gift shop sporting the carved moose on the sidewalk.

A couple hours passed and after several purchases, they loaded the bags into the back of Steve's car.

"Let's go grab some lunch. There's a great café around the corner."

"Good idea. I'm starved. Shopping makes

me hungry."

~*~

Steve sipped his coffee, staring across the table at her. *Something is different.* And he liked it. The fun had returned. *Thank you, God, thank you, God.*

"So what's next on the agenda?" Her smile lit up her face.

"Let's walk around back and see how the ice castles are forming."

"I heard about those. Who would have thought about putting out sprinklers in the winter? I saw a story on the news about them. They're really cool. Well...no pun intended. Not really anyway."

"Well, come on. Let's go." Steve handed his credit card to the server. Once he signed the receipt, they headed around the corner to the River Walk Park. The sun warmed them nicely despite them being surrounded by snow. At the entrance to the ice castle exhibit, he paid the fee.

"Oh, my goodness..." Ronnie loved looking at all the formations the sprays of water had formed. The blue sheen of the frozen water glowed from within the formations in the sunlight. It truly was a remarkable sight. Steve chanced taking her hand.

They walked together enjoying the view and the day.

"This is just beautiful."

Steve loved the look of awe on her face. She had no idea how beautiful she was. He enjoyed the frozen creations, too, but seeing the joy on her face far surpassed what the ice had done.

"Oh, Steve, I'm so glad you brought me here. I love this!"

"Go stand over there and I'll get your picture."

Ronnie rushed over to a closet size area within the walls of ice and posed.

Steve kept shooting pictures.

A woman came up next to Steve. "I could take a picture of you both if you'd like."

"Oh, thanks. That'd be great." Steve passed the camera over to her and showed her how to use it.

They had to get very close in the cold, cramped area. The warmth of happiness could have melted the ice. He put his arm around her and she leaned in against him for the picture.

"There you go. Come and check it and make sure you like it."

Steve didn't really want to leave the space he shared with Ronnie. He loved being able to hug her again. He checked the photo and knew he would forever treasure that one. "Thank you so much for taking that."

"No problem. Have fun."

"Let me see." Ronnie peered at the photo. "Oh, fun. I love that."

"Come on. Let's keep going and check this

place out some more."

They walked hand-in-hand on the pathways that wound through the display, mesmerized by the different aspects of the frozen sculptures. They were nearing the end.

"Oh, too bad. That is so fun. I'd love to see this at night with the lights sometime. We'll have to come back."

Ronnie smiled at him and fireworks went off in his heart. "Yeah, we should." It was all Steve could do to hold back his excitement of a day spent with her.

They headed back for the car on Main Street.

"So now we have choices. Tubing or sightseeing. Your choice."

"Hmmmm....are you talking the adventure park back in Frisco?"

"Yep."

"Oh, my. Tubing? I haven't done that in years. I guess we could try. I haven't been to the park yet. It looks fun. It wasn't very crowded when we drove by this morning."

"It might be now that the afternoon temps have gone up."

Driving back north on Highway 9, they saw up ahead the parking lot for the park. It was packed. The line of people for the tubing run was visible from the road.

"Look at the line!" Ronnie groaned. "I'm rethinking this idea."

Steve laughed. "Wow. I think every

teenager from Denver is up here today. That place is busy."

"So can I change my mind to that sightseeing idea?"

"You bet. Let's turn around." Steve went back a couple of miles to the stop light at the south end of Dillion Reservoir. He turned off to the left to head up the steep hill on Swan Mountain Road. He loved the overlook at Sapphire Point and thought that would give them a chance to talk.

"I know where you're going. I love that spot. I'm so glad we're doing this today. And it's so beautiful out." She leaned forward in her seat, observing the landscape and the mountains in the distance.

He pulled into the lot.

Only one other car was parked there, and a couple came up the path toward the lot.

He was glad they would be alone.

Ronnie put her hat on and pulled gloves out of a pocket.

He rushed around the car to open her door.

The sky held no clouds and the blue was so striking that it held his gaze for a moment while he waited for her to pull those gloves on.

She grinned at him, hair wisping around her hat. She was beautiful and a much better view.

The path headed alongside a triangle fence of lodge pole pines. The hillsides held the remains of cut down trees.

"What happened? This used to be all forest along the path."

"Beetle kill got over on this side; they lost every lodge pole pine. Sure opened up the view to the lake. I have friends who own a guest ranch south of here called High Country Safaris. They're starting to see the effects of the beetles, too. My buddy, Jon, worries about fires moving through. Those bugs killed so many trees."

"Wow. It's devastated." Looking around at the remains of the woods, she tripped on a root raised up from so many footsteps wearing away the trail.

Steve caught her, steadied her, and then took her hand in his. Even through the gloves, he felt the electricity he had missed these last three years.

They walked along the quarter mile trail, holding hands, to the overlook surrounded by a stone wall about knee height.

He was glad she hadn't let go.

"Oh, look! How funny. A couch made out of rock." Ronnie rushed over to the large rock about the size of a loveseat that had been carved out enough for three thin people to sit on. She brushed some remaining snow off the seat area and plopped down.

Steve pulled out his camera and took a picture of her with the few remaining ponderosa pines as a back drop. He chuckled at her exaggerated smile, walked over, and then sat next to her.

"It's so beautiful here," Ronnie whispered.

"It sure is." Steve could only stare at her.

Her gaze locked on his own.

After that moment of time thawed away, he said, "I'm glad you came."

"Me, too."

He chanced putting his arm around her, gently resting his hand on her opposite shoulder.

They stared out at the mountains to the west. The snow-covered lake sparkled like diamonds in the sunshine four hundred feet below.

When she leaned closer to him, his heart skipped a beat.

A chubby chipmunk hopped up on the rock wall near them, chirping for food.

"Look at that guy." She pointed and chuckled.

"I had a feeling…" Steve removed his arm and reached in his pocket. When he handed her a few peanuts, her eyebrow raised.

"Do you always carry peanuts with you?"

"Only for special occasions. Unsalted, of course. I hoped we could stop here today."

She snapped the shell, releasing the nuts, and leaned forward, holding one out.

The chipmunk sat up on its hind legs fidgeting with indecision. It dashed over, hesitantly took the offered nut between its teeth, and darted away. Stopping at a safe distance, it sat on its haunches again and used paws to turn the nut around and around, chewing on the edges until shoving it into his expandable cheek.

A loud squawk caught their attention. A Stellar Jay spread its long blue wings and landed on the wall. Its black head with a crest of feathers tipped from side to side looking for a treat.

"They always know when food comes around." Steve tossed a whole peanut over near the bird, which rapidly hopped over to snatch it away. It flew off to the top of a dead tree and pounded it open to eat the contents.

"I really love it up here." Ronnie sighed and leaned back into Steve again.

"I haven't seen you this relaxed in a long time."

"It's been a long time since I've felt relaxed. Kelly's been helping me a lot."

"Want to tell me about it?"

Ronnie looked off into the distance and sighed heavily.

Steve felt as if he'd intruded. "You don't have to. I'm sorry."

"No, no. It's OK. I do want to talk to you about it, but I don't know where to start."

"Start where you're at right now."

She breathed in deeply. "I've been really mad at God these last few years."

Steve nodded his head and looked down at his shoes.

"Kelly's helping me get beyond that. Showing me that it isn't God's fault that Dad died in that fire." Her gaze drifted off toward the mountains again. "Or yours, for that matter. I guess I'm trying really hard to see the truth in it all."

"It can't be easy."

"No, it's definitely not. It really shook me up when Mom told me she'd been mad at Dad. I couldn't understand it. I just couldn't bring myself to the point of seeing he was responsible for his actions and decisions that day. That God didn't do it to him." She paused and hung her head. "I've got a long way to go yet, though."

Steve pulled her closer. "I'll help you in any way I can. You know that, right?"

She looked up at him and smiled. "I know. I appreciate it. I'm sorry for pushing you away all this time. I was scared. Still am a bit. But I'm working on it."

"It's OK."

They snuggled in again and admired God's creation laid out before them. The snow-covered mountains, the hillsides leading up to them, the chattering critters...but nothing as beautiful as the woman leaning her head against his shoulder. Finally, once again, back where he wanted her to be.

17

Ronnie started to get fidgety. "I think my rear is frozen. I hate to kill a moment, but this rock is cold."

"Yeah, I guess we should move on." Steve hopped up and took her hand. "Off to Keystone!"

"Keystone?"

"Yep. You did bring skates…"

"Oh, yeah. You do realize it's been a while since I've done that, too."

"You haven't done much lately, have you?"

"Just working and studying."

He pulled her up off their rock loveseat which had a completely new meaning to her now.

Hand-in-hand, they headed back on the snow covered trail to the car.

She loved ice skating, but really hoped she didn't fall flat on her face and make a fool of herself.

Taking a left, Steve drove down the other side of Swan Mountain Road until it caught up to Highway 6.

The afternoon sun began its descent behind the mountains to the west. They still had daylight, but it wasn't direct sunshine any more.

She was kind of disappointed, knowing it would start getting colder. But Steve had done a good job of warming her heart today, so she hung onto those thoughts. Why had she turned her back on him for so long?

Keystone was decorated for the holiday in a big way. Garland, lights, and festive décor lined the streets and storefronts. They made their way to the five-acre lake.

"Wouldn't it be fun to own one of those condos?" She pointed to the buildings lining one side of the lake. "Come out and skate every day."

"I know. It'd be great. Did you know this is the largest outdoor ice rink that's maintained by a Zamboni in all of North America?"

She laughed. "No kidding? That's a crack up."

"No pun intended?"

Her hand covered her mouth as she laughed harder. "This ice best not be cracking up when I get out there."

They sat on the bench on the edge of the lake and put on their skates. "I think it's cold enough that it won't be an issue. Unless you fall too hard." Steve took off fast on his skates with a grin spread wide on his face.

She tried to slap his shoulder, but slapped air. "Funny guy."

"Come on. It's like riding a bike. It'll come back to you." The show-off skated backwards, taunting her onto the rink. He zoomed away,

She stood, keeping one hand on the bench

until she was scooped into his arms from behind. She wobbled but his grip never wavered. Shifting her, his hands steadied her at the waist. Her arms went straight out to the sides for balance. Her confidence strengthened, and she slid a foot forward, then the other.

Steve let go. He skated in front of her, turning to face her and took her hands.

Together they floated around the lake, the multi-colored lights of the Christmas tree in the center of the lake brightening as the sun went down further. The distant mountains faded from view in the twilight.

Although not alone on the rink, she imagined them to be.

Words weren't even needed. They *swooshed* across the ice developing a rhythm. A rhythm she could get used to. It felt right again.

Steve held her right arm out, his other arm wrapped snuggly at her waist, matching legs taking the same glide each time, they were dancing together as one. It was like riding a bike. He turned her in a circle and she never wavered. Smoothly, they spun circles as the music played over the loud speakers.

The magic of the moment astounded her. Tears formed in her eyes. Emotions caught up in her throat. This. This was her new Christmas. This had to become the memory she needed to move on.

~*~

It was heavenly, moving across the lake with her in his arms. Whatever God was up to in her heart, Steve loved it and didn't want this moment to end. "Are you having a good time?" He spoke into her ear.

She leaned her head against his. "Yes, I am."

As he guided her into a spin, he noticed a tear on her cheek. "Are you crying?"

She giggled. "Yes, I am."

"Do you have anything else to say?"

"Yes, I do." She let go of his hold and took off ahead. Arms outstretched, she went into a spin on her own. He remembered how good she used to skate. Then, reaching out again, she raised one leg behind her, leaned forward, and spun. She skated beautifully. As she circled back toward him, her face lit up with a smile that spread wide. The cold air tinged her cheeks pink.

He took her hand and pulled her to him. They stood there staring into each other's eyes for what seemed like forever. He wanted it to be forever. He leaned over, slowly nearing her lips with his own, unsure of what her response would be.

She tipped her head and began to close the gap.

He thought the ice would melt beneath them.

Just before their lips met, a scream punctuated the air, stealing the moment away.

18

The sound brought Ronnie back to reality.

A teenage boy lay on the ice not far from them.

People started to circle around him.

Steve and Ronnie rushed over.

"What happened?" Steve asked as they began to assess him.

"Owwww…my ankle!"

Steve checked his ankle. As he stabilized it, he whispered to Ronnie what he found. "It feels loose. Keep him calm and distracted."

"Someone call for an ambulance!" Ronnie shouted to those gathering around the commotion.

Ronnie scooted near the young man's side. "What's your name?"

"Brian. Where's my dad?" He continued to cry out in pain.

A man skated up to them. "Brian, are you OK?

"Are you his father?" Ronnie looked up at the man.

"Yes."

"We're medics. We need to get something under him and take him off the ice before shock sets in. Give me your jacket." Her stern order prompted several jackets to come flying off around them. She started the head to toe survey. With her glove off, she felt behind Brian's head and found blood, which prompted another yelp. She repositioned herself with both knees near his head.

"Steve, head injury."

"OK," Steve looked at the gathered crowd. "We need to get these jackets under him away from the ice. We're going to roll him. I need you, Dad, to roll him up, you two slide the jackets under him—carefully." He pointed to the dad and two other men.

The dad skated around to the other side of his son.

With Steve holding the leg, Ronnie gripped each side of the teen's head. She nodded at everyone, "On my count. One, two, three…" Ronnie held his head firmly to move the head in alignment with the body.

The dad gently rolled him up, jackets rapidly slid under the boy who screamed out again.

"Easy, easy. OK, back down."

"Brian, we're going to leave your skate on for now. But you need to try to calm down. The ambulance will be here soon." Steve kept a firm grip on the leg with one hand, checking the bones up to the knee with the other.

Sirens wailed as the ambulance neared the lake. Manpower would arrive with the local fire department, too. The ambulance team made their way onto the ice taking baby steps all the way. Firefighters followed behind with a backboard.

"We're with fire and rescue down the mountain. He's got a likely tib/fib break and a head injury," Steve told them.

The paramedic set the large medical bag on the ice and removed a neck brace. Splint material was next. The splint was put in place and wrapped, skate included. The other medic got the neck brace on. Once everything was stabilized, a fireman brought the backboard over. The medics took over the patient roll and he was strapped down to the board, then lifted onto the gurney. As their feet slipped and slid, they wheeled Brian off the ice to the safety of the rubber mat.

The crowd of people had disbursed and gone back to skating. Those who'd thrown their jackets down shook the snow off and quickly put them back on.

"Thanks for the help." Ronnie smiled at the remaining group.

"Thank you. Good job," echoed around the small group of people.

"Well, that was unexpected." Steve took one of her hands.

"Poor kid. He's got a long recovery ahead." She brushed the snow off the knees of her jeans.

He wrapped his arm around her and snuggled her against him. "I'm just wondering..."

She looked up at him. "What?"

"Where were we?"

She laughed, dug the tip of her skate into the ice, and took off fast.

He skated after her, laughing, too.

19

Steve was thrilled. A second special day with Ronnie within a week. Not only had he spent a day with her sight-seeing and skating; now they headed to the slopes with the Hockes.

She was trying hard to come to terms with a relationship with God and him. Experience had taught him that bitterness could grow and become exaggerated. And it had caused her so much heartache. But that time seemed to be ending.

The drive to Loveland Ski area with Kyle, Kelly, and Stephanie was beautiful and entertaining. The young girl talked endlessly, making Steve smile and nod his head a lot. She sat in her car seat between him and Ronnie, talking a mile a minute to everyone for the hour drive.

"So, Stephanie," Steve broke in when the girl took a breath. "How good of a skier are you?"

"Oh, I'm not very good, but I like it."

"Maybe I can help you today."

"That would be fun." The girl turned her upper body against the seat restraints. "Miss Ronnie, do you ski really good?"

"No, not really. It's been a while since I've

been on the mountain. I'll bet you ski better than me."

Giggles erupted. When her dad took the exit for Loveland, Stephanie screamed, "We're here."

"Stephanie! What have I told you about screaming while daddy is driving?"

"Sorry." She looked contrite until her eyes met Steve's, then her smile came back. Her legs bounced in her excitement to get out of the car. She strained against the straps of the seat.

"Hold on there." Steve put a hand on her knee. "Your dad needs to park the car before you can get out of that seat."

The little girl slammed back into the seat with an exaggerated huff.

Once parked, Ronnie got out and stretched.

Steve kept an eye on her as he unbuckled Stephanie. "Let's get your jacket back on before you get out."

Stephanie was so excited that she flapped her arms, trying to get the coat on to get out of the car.

It proved quite a challenge for Steve.

Finally, she stood and made her way for the door, pushing him aside.

Ronnie and Kyle were getting the skis out of the rack on top of the car while Kelly corralled Stephanie. Steve helped Kyle work on the sets that were on his side, half staring at Ronnie's beautiful face. He sure loved that color of blue on her.

It took extra time to get on the slopes with a child, a stop at the restroom priority number one for the girl, but Steve found himself enjoying her antics. Her excitement became contagious.

Ronnie and Steve agreed to stay on the bunny hill for a while since Stephanie would be on that all day.

Steve made it to the top of the beginner's hill with Ronnie. They turned and waited for the family to join them. It felt so good to be standing next to her.

Stephanie giggled and laughed. Her excitement over four doting adults giving her undivided attention was infectious. Fun bubbled through their little group as they whipped up and down the bunny slope.

"Why don't you two go hit some other trails? There's no reason you need to hang with us the entire day. Go have some fun."

Ronnie leaned on her poles. "Steve, do you want to try another run?"

"Sure, but no moguls for me. The ankle is a lot better, but I think the mogul run would do me in."

"I know for sure it would do me in. Let's head over to the Lower Creek Trail next to the tunnel." She pointed to the Eisenhower/Johnson tunnel on I-70.

"Sounds great." Steve lifted one ski over, then matched the other to it and pushed with his poles. "I'll race you to the chair."

"Hey, wait a minute," Ronnie hollered as she tried to catch up.

~*~

Ronnie raced, finally reaching his side. One good push sent her ahead of him. She turned to look over her shoulder and saw him dig in harder in an attempt to pass her. She pushed on even more, narrowly missing a skier who stood looking up the hill. A light snow started to fall. She spun and slid to a stop at the end of the line for lift number two. "Beat ya."

Steve had slowed and his skies glided to a stop next to her. "You cheated."

"Now you sound like Stephanie."

Steve laughed.

Familiar twinges of anxiety popped up, but Ronnie squashed them. Deep in her heart she had to stop allowing the loss of her dad affect how she lived her life. Steve helped her so much and getting back into the Bible had helped the most. She started to admit she still loved him, but old habits attempted to squelch that idea.

The chair lift came so they glided into position, sat down, the chair swung, and then rose up causing her stomach to flutter as they headed up the mountain.

Although a light snow fell, there were still a few patches of blue overhead in some areas.

Ronnie looked at the view and marveled. "What a beautiful day."

"Beautiful is right." He was looking at her, warmth glowing in his eyes.

Her face grew hot. "So, is your foot doing OK?" She had to change his focus. That look…it could turn this day into river rafting down a mountain instead of skiing.

"Yeah, it's good. I wondered how it would handle the day, but it seems fine." He looked off to their right. "This view always amazes me. I'm so glad you invited me today."

"I'm glad, too. Kyle and Kelly have been bugging me to come skiing. I thought this would be a good opportunity for us to talk and just have fun together."

"Good decision." He set his gloved hand on top of hers. "I'm glad you were willing."

The chair reached the top, and they skied off to the right of the lift. The Lower Creek Trail looped around and would give them a long, gentle ride. Being one of the easiest trails made it perfect for what they wanted to do today. They'd have to cross a few trails to meet up with the one they wanted.

Hopefully today she would let go of the past and be able to grasp the idea of a future with this man. Ronnie's heart seemed to skip a beat as she looked over at him.

His form was perfect as he skied, especially for someone who had a foot injury. His athletic ability just enhanced how handsome she found him, now that she would admit it.

"Hey, let's shoot across here." He pointed

with his ski pole toward the South Shoots. "We can catch up to the Lower Creek Trail this way."

"Want to race again? Maybe you could win this time."

Without a word, he dug in with his poles and flew off.

She dug in and followed, laughing.

"I've got you this time." When he turned to look back at her, his ski caught a snowboarder's rut. Not prepared for it, he fell face first into the snow.

She slid sideways to a stop to check on him.

Steve pushed up and the laughter started. The goggles and his mouth were packed with snow. He spit and sputtered as he tried to clear his face with his glove, ski pole stuck out to the side. He raised the goggles to his forehead. One ski had fallen off; the other put his leg at an odd angle. He pulled upright on the one and began sliding over to retrieve the other.

She couldn't help the laughter. Then she noticed that look in his eyes.

"Steve…don't…you…dare," she swung her ski around to escape. A large snowball smacked her square in the back. She turned, glancing his way.

He had attached the ski back onto his boot.

She dug deep in the sticky snow, gathered up a handful and whipped it towards him making contact on the top of his head.

"Wanna play dirty, eh?" He skied over fast, grabbed her around the waist and tackled her to the ground in the deep powder which poofed a cloud of it around them.

They both pushed their way up laughing. Skis stuck upward in complete disorder.

Ronnie had to wipe the snow off her face now.

Steve reached over and brushed it out of her bangs that now hung heavy and straight. He leaned closer, and then lowered his face to hers.

A nervous, quiet chuckle escaped her throat. Her mind told her to flee. Get on her skis and fly down the mountain, away from these feelings as fast as she could go, but her heart wanted to give in.

Her heart won.

She tentatively leaned into him, fighting the struggle within to keep her distance, but she couldn't fight this. Her attraction to him had grown stronger. She gave in to the moment and allowed his kiss to fill her spirit and warm her soul. Drops of melting snow landed on their connected lips. The moment seemed to last forever. All of her fears melted away. The world around her stopped. No one else existed. The fears of her past were gone. The dread, doubts, and worries all but disappeared as she melted into his embrace.

20

Christmas Eve, Steve, Ted, Troy, and Brian were on duty at the fire station.

Steve had volunteered because he had plans for Christmas Day.

The emergency tone disrupted. The dispatcher stated "house fire" and the address.

"That's Kelly and Kyle's place," Steve told the others.

Ted drove while the other three slipped into their self-contained breathing apparatus—SCBA—that were attached to the seat back. It saved time when they got to the scene to already be prepared. From the information the dispatcher relayed, they would need every minute.

Ted rounded the next curve.

Smoke was pouring out of a side window as flames shot into the air.

Kelly knelt outside the front door, desperately inhaling air even as coughs shook her body.

Steve ran to her. "Is everyone out?"

"Stephanie!" She coughed, gasping for breath, the soot covering her face. "She's still in there. I couldn't get to her. Kyle's not home. Please, Steve. Save her. She's in her room." Kelly gripped his arm, tears tracking down her cheeks, even as she spasmed into another coughing fit.

Brian and Troy were pulling the hose toward the house.

Ted connected the coupler to the water source and flipped switches to charge the hose as more firefighters pulled up.

"House fully engulfed. Child trapped inside." Steve yelled into the radio on his jacket,

Troy ran to the house and broke in the door. Alone. Thick black smoke flew out the door.

"Troy, don't!" Steve hollered. But the noise of the fire and the diesel truck drowned him out. *That idiot.*

Brian joined him at the hose and they charged the door.

Search and rescue. Finding Stephanie was their first priority.

Troy had air wherever he was.

The Christmas tree was fully engulfed in flames, as were the curtains.

Steve and Brian gave a quick, five-second burst of water from the attack line they held. "Up the stairs to the right." Steve yelled.

Both men dropped to their knees to function below the thick smoke that filled the rest of the room. In the dense fog, Steve couldn't see much of anything, nor any sign of Troy.

Steve and Brian crawled up the stairs, dragging the charged hose with them. Crawl, pull, set it down, repeating the action all while not being able to see a thing.

Steve gritted his teeth hard thinking of Troy's foolishness. They had to find Steph first. She had no chance against the killer smoke.

Troy would hopefully realize his stupidity and get back out of the house.

Steve hoped he would, anyway. He didn't want to have to hunt for him, too. The search process ran a gamut of emotions and exhaustion. Being in the lead, Steve felt along the walls for the door.

Smoke billowed up the stairwell obscuring their vision even more. They had to rely on their other senses. *I have to find her. Please Lord, let her be all right.*

~*~

Ronnie arrived with the rescue squad.

The ambulance pulled in behind them.

Other firefighters were on the scene and attacking the flames that shot through the side window licking the nearby trees.

George, the fire chief, stood holding Kelly back as she fought to run toward the house. She screamed, pummeled George on the chest, and then coughed as if it were her last breath.

Ronnie ran toward them with the portable oxygen.

Kelly bent forward, hands on her knees in an attempt to clear her smoke-filled lungs.

"George, let's get her over to the ambulance." Ronnie fought the swinging arms of her friend to place the O2 mask on Kelly's face, slipping the rubber band around to the back of her head. "Kelly, keep this on." Ronnie got right in Kelly's face with the order.

"No," she screamed. "My baby's in there. Ronnie, I have to go to her." Kelly's eyes were wide with fear.

A hose line snaked in the door and smoke was pouring out. Ronnie's heart sank *Stephanie is in there.* That sweet little girl they had so much fun with on the ski slopes. "The guys will get her. Come on. You need oxygen. You can't do anything to help. Let's take care of you, so you can help her when they get her out."

George wrapped an arm around Kelly's waist. "Steve will get her, Kelly."

Ronnie turned back and looked at the flames consuming the west end of the home. *Steve is in there?* Fear engulfed her heart. He wouldn't stop until he found the child. A million thoughts raced as she fought to stay in control of emotions.

The fear from her father's loss reared up. Her stomach twisted as she envisioned Steve's funeral. She couldn't move. The increasing heat from the flames eating away at her friend's home warmed her face, but dreadful cold seeped through her gear. Snapping, popping noises seemed to echo in the air. The pungent smell of the swirling smoke twisted. Carrying its scent to her nose. Fire, destructive, all-consuming fire.

George's yell broke through her distracted thoughts. "Ronnie! Come on."

She shook her senses back into place and moved. She took Kelly's other arm and led her to the waiting ambulance.

Kelly sat on the pram, her fear-filled eyes stared, the tears causing rivers of soot as they ran down her face. Her coughs attempted to rid her body of the toxic invader. The smoke continued to roll like fog over a mountain top out of the windows and the door the attack line went in.

Ronnie, Kelly, and George all stood watching. Waiting.

A vehicle pulled in behind them. Kyle practically fell out and ran toward the ambulance.

"Ronnie." Then he saw his wife. "Oh, my gosh, Kelly." He enveloped her in a protective hug. Looking around the area, his eyes went wide. "Where's Stephanie?"

Ronnie's eyes teared up at the thought of Stephanie in that smoking fire all alone. Her jaw wobbled, but she squelched the emotions. She had to be strong.

Kelly pulled the mask off as she threw her arms around Kyle. "I couldn't get to her. She's still in there." Wrenching sobs wracked her body.

Kyle pulled from her grasp and turned to run.

George stepped in front of Kyle and put a firm hold on his arms. "Let them do the job, Kyle. You know you can't go in there."

"My daughter's in there. Let me go!" Kyle fought against his boss, but it was useless with the hold George had on him.

~*~

It seemed like hours, but only seconds had gone by. Precious, life-giving and life-taking seconds. *Find Stephanie's room. I've been to the house. Stephanie dragged me up to see her room. I know where it is. Find it.* He crawled up the stairs along the wall. *Her room is the first door to the right.*

The door was closed. He turned the knob, but it was difficult to open. Something blocked it. "Stephanie!"

He shoved against it. The smoke quickly filled the room ending his ability to see. His hand discovered a blanket, but no girl was bundled in it. The blanket was what hindered getting the door open. *Good girl!* She'd blocked the crack under the door, just as her firefighter father had obviously taught her.

"Stephanie," his voice sounded muffled in the mask. He called louder as he crawled around the room.

She wasn't under the bed or anywhere on the floor.

"Stephanie, where are you?" The noise of the fire's destruction, the trucks outside, the spray from the hoses hitting the house with pressurized water and the sound of his frantic heartbeat filled his ears. The gray-filled room made it impossible to see anything. "Stephanie." He found her closet door. "Stephanie!" A memory teased in his brain. *"See my princess gowns?"* Stephanie had flung open her closet door and shown him her prized possessions. He turned the knob and she fell out against his arm. A blanket covered her small body.

"Uncle Steve?" the child's raspy voice was music to his ears. She coughed and grabbed at him.

He hugged her against his chest, blanket and all. His heart was in his throat, and tears leaked a little. He'd found her. *Thank you, God.* Hunched over his precious cargo, he felt along the wall to get out of the room.

Brian put a hand on his shoulder, acknowledging he was right behind them. Steve turned and ran through the thickening smoke, desperate to get Stephanie to safety, to her frantic parents. He followed the hose line out the door. Brian burst out after him.

Another team battled the blaze.

Once outside, Stephanie continued coughing.

Thank you God. He removed the blanket that covered her. "You OK, Steph?"

"You saved me, Uncle Steve." She flung her arms around Steve's neck setting his helmet askew. She coughed more.

Tears welled up again. "You did well, Steph. You blocked that door just like you're supposed to." He swallowed, his heart back in his chest, his thankfulness to God so intense that he felt wrung out.

"I 'membered." Coughing robbed the rest

of her sentence.

He handed her to a waiting firefighter.

Kyle ran up and grabbed his daughter up in a hug that was almost heartbreaking, his relief was so plain on his face.

The captain was right behind him.

"Where's Troy? Did he get out?" Steve asked George.

"We can't raise him on the radio. He's still in there. Greg and Matt are in looking for him."

Steve ran back towards the door. He tapped Brian with the back of his hand and waved him into the inferno.

~*~

A firefighter brought Stephanie over to the waiting ambulance.

Kelly threw off her mask and engulfed her daughter in a hug. She patted the girl down, as if making sure that every bit of Stephanie had made it outside.

Covered by black smudges, Stephanie coughed violently.

"Baby, baby, are you OK?" Kelly brushed the hair back from her child's face.

"Uncle Steve saved me." Then coughing took over.

Ronnie assessed the child for burns while the paramedic got the pediatric oxygen mask in place. Once she was ready, they loaded both mother and child into the ambulance, which then took off, siren screaming. Kyle followed in his car kicking up gravel as he chased after his wife and child.

Ronnie wanted to thank Steve for saving Stephanie but she didn't see him. The whole area was lit from the emergency flood lamps. She scanned the entire scene, not seeing Steve at all.

George spoke into the radio and requested another ambulance.

Ronnie rushed up to George. "Where's Steve?" Panic began to well up in her gut.

"He went back in after Troy."

Her head whipped toward the still burning house.

Thick black smoke rose and whirled around the tree tops intermingled with snaking flame.

"No. Please God, not again."

21

Steve led as he and Brian searched for Troy on their hands and knees.

Troy's carelessness would enrage the chief. The man's future as a firefighter was probably doomed. Being reckless in such a dangerous situation, never accepting protocol, this would do him in. If the fire hadn't already.

Steve was as angry as he was fearful for Troy's life.

Water sprayed over them. Blackness overpowered the path ahead. The radios sputtered with talk as the other search team went up to the second floor. Steve and Brian crawled their way to the kitchen, staying close together in the search.

Steve desperately tried to remember the layout. He hadn't been in their house for long the day they all went skiing. There was an open stair well to the lower level of the house. He felt for the opening. "I'm going down!" he hollered to Brian. At the bottom of the stairs, Steve bumped into a leg.

Troy's helmet no longer protected his head and the mask sat cock-eyed on his face.

"Troy," he yelled. Checking for

consciousness and finding none, Steve quickly set the mask back in place so Troy would get air.

"Let's get him out of here," Brian said.

Steve hoisted Troy over his shoulder.

Brian led the way as they rushed to escape the burning home.

~*~

Memories flooded Ronnie's brain. The day they got the news about her father's death. Visions of her Steve-decorated apartment. Steve tossing her into the snow on the slopes. The fun they had with little Stephanie, the ice-skating, all jumbled together in her mind.

He had to make it out. She could not bear to lose another. Why was she in this business? Why had she allowed herself to care about a firefighter? She knew better. The chance of losing him to a fire had better odds. It could happen this night, right before her eyes.

Ronnie chewed her lower lip, and her hands worked around each other in a wrestling match of fingers. Pacing in the driveway proved futile, but she had to keep moving. Tears began to escape. Traitorous tears that proved she had indeed fallen back in love. It could not be denied. Yet it had to be. Especially now.

George moved close. "Ronnie, I can't tell you not to worry, but trust his abilities. He's a great firefighter. He's not alone, and I don't mean just Brian being with him."

"My dad wasn't alone, either." Her voice came out less than a whisper and she was unable to remove her gaze from the burning home.

George reached up and put an arm around her shoulders.

She barely felt the comfort.

His radio crackled and he stepped away as he spoke back into it.

She stood, waiting for some sign, some relief, the endless torment in her heart pulling at her stomach, turning it inside out. Her knees began to wobble. Tears flowed freely. Her ears no longer processed sound—as if someone had pressed the mute button.

Thick white smoke now rose into the tree tops instead of the black killer. White or black. It didn't matter.

She knew all too well any color of smoke could be deadly. Life went into slow motion.

Crews on the outside sprayed water onto the dark, rough openings that used to be a section of roof over the back corner of the house. One hose line lay in the doorway, occasionally moving side to side with great effort as if a giant python struggled to eat its prey.

The smoke began changing as it poured out the front door. The billowing killer roiled and parted.

Ronnie's heart rate kicked up higher with hope.

A foot broke through the curtain of smoke first. A firefighter flung over another's shoulder.

Who was it?

She took slow, heavy steps forward, straining to see.

A pair of firefighters broke through the heavy veil emerging into the clear air.

Paramedics with their gear and a pram were suddenly running past her.

All the noises returned. She ran toward them. Training kicked in. She had to help.

Steve. It had to be Steve.

The injured firefighter was being lowered onto the gurney. Paramedics fumbled against the soot blackened man who had carried him out. His helmet was knocked off.

"Steve!" She ran to him.

He stepped back allowing the paramedics to take care of the patient.

Her arms flew up and around his neck awkwardly finding a way around the mask, air hose, and tank which rested on his back.

~*~

"Ronnie," Steve wrapped an arm around her. With the other hand, he pulled off the mask and dropped it. His breaths were short and rapid after carrying Troy out of the home.

Sobs racking her body.

The noise of the diesel trucks running, the hoses spraying, shouts of the crews battling the blaze, all of it seemed to fade away.

"I'm OK." He stroked her hair gathering it

at the base of her neck raising her face to his. He cupped the back of her head and looked in her eyes.

"I was so scared..." Her gaze went back to the fire, then returned to him, as if trying to determine if he was really standing there.

"It's OK." He lowered his face to kiss her lips and calm her heart.

Her hands came up against his chest stopping his motion. She stared into his eyes again, then pushed away. She turned and ran back to the truck.

Troy started coughing.

Steve stared at Ronnie moving away from him, and then returned his attention to the paramedic as he administered oxygen to Troy. "Is he all right?"

"Took in a lot of smoke, but I think you got to him in time. We'll get him to the hospital and see how he does."

Steve fell into place at the back end of the pram, helping to push it through the sloppy snow toward the waiting ambulance. He assisted them in loading the patient into the back, then stepped away. He looked at the rescue truck. Ronnie's face was lit from the surrounding lights in the side mirror. Her arm rested on the door frame with her hand partially covering her mouth.

He didn't know what to do. He understood she had been scared. But he was fine. Obviously. Why would she still be shaken up?

The ambulance lights came on as it pulled

out onto the road and took off with Troy. The siren pierced the air, circulating colored lights bounced off the landscape of pine trees.

The smoke from what was left of the house was very light now as the crews finished spraying. The cleanup poles with hooks reached from the inside, pulling down the now charred ceiling, followed by debris coming out the window. Time for mop up.

His fellow firefighters needed his help. He headed toward the half shell of Kyle's home. Reality for them now meant no Christmas, no decorated home, little Stephanie's presents would be completely gone.

From Kyle's and Kelly's interaction with everyone, they were thankful they were all alive. Especially their daughter.

Thoughts of when she'd fallen into his arms out of the closet made his eyes moisten again. She'd followed her father's instructions precisely, and her own actions had more to do with saving her life than his did. He'd simply gone in after her. He walked toward the door, thinking one day, he'd train any children he had to do the same. Despite her emotionally charged distance at the moment, he thought of the ring he still had hidden at home and dared to hope Ronnie would be their mother, too.

~*~

Relieved, Ronnie watched him walk to the

house. She was done. Now for sure. This relationship ended as of right now. She would not take the risk of seeing something like this again. She couldn't face the possibility of losing him like she'd lost her dad. This had been too close to home for her.

I am with you. Trust Me.

What did that mean?

I will not forsake you.

She shook her head.

Where the team worked, Steve was helping to carry smoldering items out of the house.

Matt climbed in the driver's seat. "I guess we're done here. Ready to go?"

"Huh? Yeah, ready." She reached over her shoulder for her seat belt and buckled in.

22

Ronnie flipped through a magazine in the waiting room of the hospital, but she couldn't really see anything on the pages. Only the memory of smoke pouring out of a home played in her mind. When she closed her eyes, she could envision Steve crawling, searching for sweet little Stephanie. The killer smoke could have claimed them both. Smoke that held the man she found herself once again falling in love with. A tear tried to escape from the corner of her eye. She flicked to the next page almost ripping it away.

They'd been told Troy would be under observation for the next couple of days.

Steve thanked the doctor.

She knew this would happen. Sure, he made it out. This time. What about the next time? She'd tried very hard to protect her heart. She had built up a solid, unbreakable wall after her Dad died. Then Steve worked his way back into her life and had to start taking her comfortable wall apart piece by piece until it couldn't hold anything back any longer. Why did she let him in? She knew better.

Steve leaned up against the wall, staring at the door. A couple of times he looked her way, but she did her best to avoid his glance.

This had to end. She couldn't fall back into the trap that would lead to nothing but heartache.

Kyle stepped through the doors with a big smile on his face. "Hey, you two. Kelly will have Steph out here in a minute. They're both fine."

Ronnie dumped the magazine onto the table in front of her chair. Rushing over, she hugged her friend. "Oh, Kyle, what a relief."

"They've had Steph on oxygen all this time, but everything looks clear in her lungs. She's feeling better. Thanks to you, Steve, she's going to be all right." Kyle stepped away from Ronnie, reached out to shake hands with Steve, pulling him into a one-armed man hug. "I don't know how I will ever repay you for saving her life, buddy."

Steve hugged him back. "Hey, man, glad we got there when we did. She's a smart little girl. She did everything right. Well, except that closet thing."

"Yeah, we're going to work on that 'get out the window' deal. If we have a home. Were you able to save any of the house?"

"Not much, Kyle."

Ronnie put a hand on Kyle's shoulder. "We're all there for you guys. If you need help, you know that both departments will do whatever is needed."

"I know. Thanks. We'll figure it out. I'll call our insurance agent and see what can be worked out."

The doors opened again and Kelly came out, carrying Stephanie.

The little girl's face lit up and she wiggled to get down from her mom's arms. She ran to Steve, who scooped her up into a hug. "Uncle Steve! You saved me. You're my hero!" She kissed his cheek, then her arms tightened around his neck, making his face go red.

Ronnie couldn't help but smile.

Steve held the girl with one arm, rubbing her hair with his other hand. "I'm so glad you're OK. I need my skiing buddy."

"Yeah." Her head bobbed up and down as she leaned back in his arms to look at him. Her nose wrinkled up. "You stink."

Steve laughed, sniffing deeply at the strong smoke smell that radiated off him and making her laugh.

Ronnie reached out for Kelly and they hugged. "Kelly, if I can do anything, please, just ask. I'm so sorry about the house."

"I assume it's gone…"

"Pretty much." Ronnie hated to tell her.

"It'll be a challenge, but just knowing that Stephanie is OK, that's all that matters to me. Stuff is stuff."

"I admire your attitude."

"Remind me of that when I actually see the place and burst into tears." Kelly squished up her expression.

~*~

Steve followed Ronnie as they walked their friends out to their car.

After hugs, the family got in and headed out to find a hotel to call home.

Steve stepped over and put his arm around Ronnie's shoulder while she waved after the car. She quickly pulled out from under his arm. He knew everything was eating at her, since she hadn't really said a word to him the whole time they waited in the hospital. He took a chance. "Are you OK?"

She looked at him with something close to ferocity. "You could have been killed. Just like my father. This is exactly why I told you I do not want to date firefighters. I can't do this Steve." Ronnie stomped away from him.

"Ronnie, come on. I'm OK. Everything worked out." He rushed to catch up to her.

She turned sharply and he ran into her. "This time!"

"All times as God chooses."

"And why did God not choose to get my father through it alive? How do I know when God is going to just let you die in one of these fires? I didn't want to fall in love with you, but now I have. I just about lost you, Steve. I can't go through it again." She headed for her truck.

Steve caught up to her, reached out and pulled her into his arms. He had no words. He just held her.

Her tears flowed freely. She sobbed

against his chest. Her fist slammed against him.

How could he explain to her to trust in the Lord with all her heart?

Snowflakes started to fall.

"Ronnie, none of us know. All our days are numbered by the Lord. Only He knows how long we'll be here on this earth. How do I know if you'll come back from the store? How do we ever know any outcome? It can happen anytime to anyone, but if we live our lives in fear of losing someone, all we've done is robbed life from the happiness of the present moment."

"You know the odds are stronger in this profession. Firefighting is one of the most dangerous occupations." She pushed away from him.

"The odds are worse for the people in trouble if we aren't there to help them. We're trained to be as safe as possible."

She went over to the hood of the truck, lowered her head onto it, crossed her arms and cried. Her body shook; he imagined it was as much from the cold as from the overpowering emotions of all the events that crashed down.

A few people stared as they headed to their cars.

Steve leaned against the truck next to her. What could he do? He loved her. He wanted to spend his life with her, but this obstacle would always be there between them, holding her back from completely loving him. He stood silently with his elbow on the hood, fingers rubbing the rough stubble on his chin.

Silent sobs shook her body.

"I'll quit."

She looked up, puzzled. "What?" Tears ran down her red tinged cheeks.

"I'll quit. I'll find a new line of work."

She turned to face him. "You know you can't do that. You love firefighting. I could never ask you to give it up."

He reached out his hand and placed it on her arm. "Understand something, Ronnie. I love you. You know I do. I will do anything if it means I can spend my life with you."

"Steve...I can't. You can't. If you weren't able to fight fires, you would hate it. You would eventually resent me for making you give up your career. No. I won't go there. This is exactly why I never wanted to get involved with you."

He leaned closer. "Then why did you?" he asked with a whisper.

She met his gaze with her own tear-filled eyes and fell against his chest.

He wrapped his arms around her.

"Because I fell in love with you."

He continued his defense quietly. "Then we need to figure out a way around this. I mean it, Ronnie. I will do anything for you."

"I know you would, Steve. But I won't ask you to give up your career."

"I could go on rescue. We'll both have our EMTs soon. We could work together all the time."

"At every fire scene, you'd be itching to

run in."

"I'll just change my priorities for the job. I'd still be helping people. Ronnie, I love you. I want to make this work."

"I don't know. I have to think about this."

"Promise me you'll pray about it. God will work things out. He's in control and wants what's best for you. That *could* be me, you know." He gave her his best debonair leer.

She stared at him for a long time. The silence was unnerving as she studied him, as if looking into his soul. That was fine, as far as he was concerned. She needed to see that he loved her with everything he had.

"Give me some time Steve. I just need to sort things out."

23

"Hi Kelly. Are you two ready to go?" Ronnie stood at the door of the hotel room where the Hockes were staying since the fire.

"Come on in. Steph's looking for her other shoe."

The room held two beds and several shopping bags sat on the floor.

"Been shopping?" Ronnie pointed to the pile.

"Yeah. Trying to get some necessities while we wait on insurance. We couldn't salvage much from the house, as you know. Our clothes were toast." Kelly laughed. "Pun intended."

"I don't know how you keep such a good attitude about this."

"Won't do me any good to feel sorry for myself. I have my moments, but for Stephanie's sake, I don't want her to get upset by it all any more than she has been. She keeps remembering the toys she no longer has. It's hard for her to understand."

"I found it, Momma." Stephanie popped up from the other side of the far bed. "Hi, Miss Ronnie." She limped over holding a shoe out. The one on her foot blinked at the heel with each step

169

she took.

Kelly knelt down to help with the shoe.

"I'm glad you can go with us, Miss Ronnie."

"Me, too, Stephanie."

"I have got to get out of this room or I'll go stir crazy. We've got to find a bigger place to rent until the house is rebuilt."

They headed out to Kelly's minivan and got Stephanie buckled into her seat.

Ronnie climbed into the passenger's side and buckled up.

"Momma said I can get a new doll. Mine got toasted."

"I know where she got that line." Ronnie laughed.

Kelly smiled and pulled out of the parking spot. "We'll stop after we look for a place to live and get your new doll, OK?"

"Yay!"

"So how are you doing, Ronnie? I haven't really talked to you since the night of the fire."

"Better than you, I imagine."

"Ronnie, I know how shook up you were when Steve was in the house."

"I'm fine. Really. Just a lot to think about."

"Like…?"

Ronnie huffed. "He says he'll give up firefighting for me."

Kelly spun her head to look at Ronnie so fast it was a wonder she could drive straight.

"Careful. You'll get whiplash."

Kelly whipped her gaze back to the road.

"Uncle Steve isn't a firefighter anymore?" The sweet voice came from the backseat.

"Honey, Ronnie and I are talking." Kelly looked at her daughter in the rear view mirror then glanced at Ronnie again. "And how do you feel about that?"

Leaning her head against the headrest, she closed her eyes as air expelled between her lips. "I don't know. Well, I do know. Steve would resent me forever if that happened. I can't let him give up a career he's worked so hard to get. He loves the job."

"I think he loves you more."

Ronnie rested her elbow against the base of the window and held her head in her hand. "I know. I'm still in love with him, too. But what if he doesn't make it out of a fire someday? How would I ever make it through that?"

"Whenever my worries start to take over, I have to remind myself of the verse in Romans eight that if my mind is controlled by the Spirit I'll have peace. I have to trust and remember the promises of God. The fire taught me even more in that area. I have to stay focused on Him right now."

"I just don't think I'm strong enough, Kelly."

"Sure you are. Do you know why?"

"Nope. Not a clue."

"By His grace. His power is made perfect in your weakness."

"I think I read that the other day, but I didn't get it."

"No matter what we go through in life, His power will shine through the trial if we stay focused on Him. But God also knows what will happen in our lives. Nothing surprises Him. He doesn't want harm to come our way. He wants our lives to have hope and a future. To get to know Him better. Maybe God is trying to tell you that you and Steve should be together. That you do have a future. Maybe you have to quit arguing with God about it."

"You don't hold back, do you?"

"I don't like to waste time. I don't like to see others do that either. Time's a-wasting, girlfriend. You've got a good man wanting to love you forever. It's time to stop worrying about what could go wrong, and focus on what could go right. I'd rather have Kyle for as many years as I can get him, than to not have him at all."

"I guess I have been a bit pessimistic about our relationship." Ronnie stared off to the meadow they drove past.

"Jesus cried with you about your dad. He loves you and when your heart breaks, His heart breaks. But think of the joy Jesus also had when He received your dad into the Kingdom. Do you think we might be showing doubt in God's goodness, though, when we linger in that sadness?"

"There's just no beating around the bush with you, is there?" Ronnie raised an eyebrow at her friend.

"Just sayin'…"

Ronnie looked out the window, contemplating all the jumbled thoughts in her head.

Kelly broke into her contemplations. "So how much confidence do you have in Steve and his abilities?"

"What? Why do you ask that?"

"Well, do you worry about losing him because he isn't good at the job?"

"No. Of course not. He's one of the best."

"Do you really believe that?"

"Kelly, you saw him that night. You know how talented he is for the job. He's not careless; he truly cares about doing it right. He saved both Stephanie and Troy. You're not really questioning his abilities, are you? After all that?"

"What if he faced a worse situation?"

"He'd do whatever he needed to. You know how rigorous the training is. And he's completely devoted to the work. He's one of the most committed at the department. They are even considering him for promotion."

"So?"

Ronnie's heart rate had increased at this line of questioning. "So. He's great at firefighting. And now with the EMT status, he'll be even better."

"Exactly!"

Ronnie's brow pinched tight looking at her friend.

"Will you ever trust God and Steve's ability, or will you always assume the worst of both of them?"

"You are one sneaky woman."

"Just want you to think about what causes you so much doubt." Kelly pulled into the driveway of a small house with a "for rent" sign out front. "Here's the first one to see today."

"Are we going to live here, Mommy?"

"I don't know yet, honey. Let's go look inside and see if we like it."

Ronnie opened the sliding side door of the van to help Stephanie out of her seat. "Come on, Sweetie. I'll carry you in." Lifting the child, she headed for the sidewalk with Kelly.

"It's kind of cute. Small...but I guess we don't need much room since we don't have much left."

They spent two more hours looking at everything from apartments to small condos, and even some older homes around town.

Kelly turned the car into the hotel lot and parked next to Ronnie's truck. "I'm done. I'll have to go over the numbers with Kyle and we'll try to decide."

"I hope you can get into something quickly. Let me know if there's anything I can do to help."

"I will, thanks. At least moving won't take much effort." Kelly laughed as she headed to their room hand in hand with Stephanie who had a brand new doll in hand.

Ronnie was amazed at Kelly's attitude. Starting the truck to let it warm, she stared out at the surrounding hills.

Last night's snow slid off the tree branches as the afternoon sun allowed the pine needles to let go of their icy coat.

Kelly had said God wanted the best for her. Now she had more to think about. Walking in the front door, she headed for the mail she'd tossed on the table earlier. "Bill, bill, no I don't want another credit card…" The bills went into a special pile, the junk mail went into the trash. The next letter in the small pile had the return address of the State of Colorado. She pulled it out, slid the other letters under her arm and opened the official-looking letter.

"Well, I'll be…I'm now an EMT." Along with the letter, were the new patches she would attach to her uniform signifying her status. She smiled with a deep sense of achievement, yet wished she could show her dad.

24

The dispatcher described the call. A climber trapped on a ledge. Thankfully, the temperatures were tolerable for this rescue.

Ronnie hopped in the passenger seat of the rig.

The rescue and fire teams got to the scene after a bit of a hike into the park, carrying all their gear, the snow just over their ankles.

One of the climber's friends met them at the fork in the trail and led the rescuers to the scene.

Up on the cliff, a young man stood facing the rock wall. His feet held to a small area of granite ledge. Icicles hung in the shady areas. Climbing the rocks was a popular sport in the area, regardless of the time of year.

"How long has he been there?" she asked the friend.

"It's been a while. We were teaching him to climb, but he hit that spot up to his right and slipped. He landed on that ledge and now we can't get him to move."

"Is he injured?"

"I don't think so, but he's so afraid, it's like he's stuck."

The fire department personnel started to arrive.

Ronnie was an experienced climber and knew rappelling, so she volunteered to lower down and rescue the individual. It took a bit to climb hauling the ropes and gear. Once perched above the victim, her partner tied off the rope securely while she put her harness on.

"Rope," her partner yelled as he flung the length over the side to warn those below.

It landed six feet to the side of the frightened young man, far enough away from his reach so he wouldn't grab it in a panic. A slight screech escaped the teen.

Ronnie hooked the rappelling mechanism onto the cold stiff rope. "Climber on," she yelled, and then took that first step over the edge. Her heart flipped a little as her feet planted against the vertical rock face, her weight full against the rope. She loved to rappel, but that first step over the top of perfectly stable rock always intimidated her.

Steve, along with the others, had taken up the belay position at the bottom.

"Great," she groaned not wanting to think about him right now.

The cliff looked to be about seventy feet with the victim at roughly twenty feet down.

She pushed out and slid down the rope four or five times before reaching the young man's level. She set the lock into place to keep from moving down the rope. "Hey, how ya doing?" She reached out to touch the young man's shoulder.

He pressed into the rock even tighter. "Don't touch me!" His red face, white knuckles, and tightly clenched eyes told the whole story. This kid was petrified.

Ronnie put her hand back on her rope. "What's your name? I want to help you get down from here."

"Joe, but leave me alone. I can't do it. I can't move."

"Well, Joe, we can't leave you here. My name is Ronnie, and I'll be helping you get down. You'll be OK. I'll make sure of it."

He ventured a peek at her, barely moving his head. His legs were shaking.

She'd seen this kind of fear before when a friend tried to cross a large log over a raging creek. His equilibrium became so challenged, he dropped down with a leg on each side of the log and sat frozen. It took more than a half an hour to coax him off that log. She'd be facing the same situation here, just dangling about fifty feet up. "Joe, are you getting cold? Don't you want to get back down to some warmth?"

"I can't." His hands dug harder into the cracks in the cold granite causing his fingertips to go white.

"Joe, listen to me. I'm coming over there to hook your harness into my rope. The guys down below have us locked in, we can just lower right on down, and then you'll be safe. OK Joe?"

"No!" His entire body shook.

"Joe, we have to get you down. You can just close your eyes and let me do all the work."

"I'll fall. I can't do this." The pitch of his voice grew higher than most young girls.

"You're not going to fall. I'll have you. Just do what I say, OK? Close your eyes." Ronnie slowly walked across the vertical rocks closer to him. She found a foothold on the small ledge he stood on. Pushing his rope aside, she hooked the locking D-ring onto the harness at his waist so that he would be tethered to her. She unlocked her rope so they could lower down. "Now you're hooked to me. You cannot fall." She explained as she worked.

Joe turned and flung his arms around her neck, knocking her off her position. They spun and twisted, four legs going in every direction.

Ronnie slammed into the rock wall, scraping her back. Her hard hat banged against the stone.

They dropped a couple of feet.

Joe let out a scream.

~*~

The rescue was going great until the young man flew against Ronnie.

Steve pulled with all his weight against the rope, locking the two instantly.

Ronnie tried to right herself, but the young man had a death grip around her neck.

Steve held firm to keep them from

plummeting down, and, even though the two whirled around like rag dolls, they didn't lose another inch of their elevation.

Ronnie struggled to turn and keep from scraping her back again while still protecting the victim.

The young man's flailing movements finally stopped.

She steadied the two of them, holding the back of the young man's belt with one hand, and touching the rock wall with the other.

"Ronnie," Steve called up to her. "Are you set? I'll start lowering you both. Just hang on."

"Lower away," she called down.

He slowly let the rope loosen through the carabineer.

She kept a hand moving down the rock to keep them steady.

As they neared the bottom, Steve could see her other hand held firm on the back of the victim's harness. Once he had them safely on the ground, he noticed the young man's forehead beaded with sweat even though the temperature had fallen below forty degrees.

The rest of the crew assisted in righting Ronnie and the victim, unhooking the two belts. They helped the victim to sit down and assessed him for any injuries.

The young man's friends gathered around.

Steve stepped back, pulling the rope the rest of the way out of the metal rings. He walked over to Ronnie as she slipped out of the harness.

"You OK?" He held out an arm for her to lean on as she stepped out of the straps.

"Yeah, I'm fine."

"Poor kid. That had to be tough for him."

"Man, he was scared. Glad you were on belay. Thanks."

"Anytime. You did a great job as usual."

~*~

She felt the heat rise in her face. "Thanks. I think that one had a bit of Divine Intervention when he flew into me." She got caught up on those last words.

Steve helped gather up the gear and then went towards the crowd around Joe, probably to check on the victim. He was always good about that, making sure rescued people were aware that he was concerned about their well-being.

Ronnie looked away and stood stock still, staring up at the cliff she had just come down.

I am with you always.

The thought startled her.

Never will I leave you; never will I forsake you.

"The Lord is my helper; I will not be afraid," she whispered. How many rescues had she been on that put her safety or her life in jeopardy? Too many to count. Yet, here she was, able to help again. Ronnie walked closer to the rock wall and reached out to touch it. She stood there in the cold shadows of the forest that crawled up against the granite boulders. The rock.

The Rock. A foundation to build on. It's unmovable. The Solid Rock where she could stand, if she allowed herself to. Just as she relied on that rope, her footing against the cliff, Christ was where her hope, her comfort, her trust, her everything should rest.

She might never understand why her dad was taken away, but he always trusted Jesus with his life. Each thought brought new delight to her mind, as if heaven opened up and poured the love and realizations into her. Truth. Why should she not trust Jesus in the loss of her father? Her dad was with Jesus right now, from the moment life left his body. He may have had a tragic end to life, but he knew where he'd spend eternity. Wasn't that eternal life better than her selfishness of holding him here? Holding his memory in her tight grip, rather than releasing it and living her life. On the Rock. What had she been doing?

She felt the sun peek through the trees pouring light on her shoulders; she was enlightened in God's truth and the warmth of the sun. His Son.

"Coming Ronnie?" She jumped when Steve spoke behind her.

"Yeah...on my way." She gathered her share of the gear and followed behind everyone down the shady, snow-tromped path. Her thoughts again went to her father.

Would he have gone in after John had he known the outcome? Would he have willingly given up his life for his partner? His friend?

She knew the answer, because she knew the man. The man who raised her and taught her the importance of life. The importance of serving. So many lessons she had forgotten in her grief. He wouldn't have wanted her living like this, avoiding love in the fear of grief.

What was wrong with her? Why had she allowed her life to go like this?

Her mother had moved on. Her brother didn't wallow in grief.

Steve had tried so hard to help her find her way out of it.

Kelly was teaching her.

And she knew, now, deep down in her heart, God was truly in control. And if He was in control, then her future in Him wasn't an ambiguous feeling to experiment with, but to find confidence of certain victory in this life and beyond. She had a lot more thinking to do. And praying.

Her dad died for a friend.

Ronnie had a Savior who died for her.

25

Ronnie accepted when Steve called for a day of snowshoeing in the nearby wilderness area. She looked forward to it, more than she dreamed possible. She watched from her patio doors for him to pull into the parking lot. With the sun shining, it would be a spectacular day. Colorado winters got cold, but with the sun shining at altitude, it made a huge difference in the temperature and the attitude.

When his vehicle turned in, she grabbed her snowshoes and headed out.

"Hi, Ronnie." Steve opened the car door for her.

"Hi." She tossed her snowshoes behind the seat and felt a longing she couldn't resist. She reached up and hugged him tight.

His look was cautious as his arms came around her.

She chuckled, not saying a word. She got in the SUV without missing a glance at his surprised face.

Steve got in and buckled up. "You're in a good mood today."

"Yep."

"Not going to tell me why?"

"Nope."

"Alrighty, then. Guess we'll head out."

Ronnie couldn't help but giggle. "I've done a lot of thinking and praying lately."

"Yeah?" Steve turned onto the main road.

"Yeah. I think I'm beginning to understand what you've been saying."

"And that is..."

"About God being in control. I realized on the climbing rescue that Dad would have gone in after John even if he knew he wouldn't survive. That's the way Dad was. He would never stand idly by when someone was in trouble."

"It was a great profession for him to be in."

"So, I've decided it's time to let go and let God take care of all my fears. When I found that verse in 1 Peter, I decided to pray it into my life. Every day I've prayed. 'I cast all my anxiety on You Lord, for You care for me.' It's really helped."

Steve's eyes went wide as he turned to stare at her, then he looked back at the road. His expression of shock was priceless. He pulled off in a wide spot off the highway and stopped.

"What's wrong?" She looked behind them to see if he was getting out of the way of another vehicle.

He got out of the car without saying a word, walked around the SUV in the sloppy snow and open her door. He held out his hand to her and motioned her to stand.

Ronnie unbuckled her seat belt and took

his hand. "Steve, what are you doing? Are you throwing me out?"

He pulled her out of the car and hugged her. One hand held the back of her head, fingers entwining in her hair, the other held her lower back. He whispered into her ear, "I've waited a long time to hear those words. You've found peace once again, haven't you?"

"Yeah, I guess I have."

They stood there holding each other.

Ronnie didn't want the moment to end.

He pulled back just a bit. "I don't really want to leave, but we're almost to the trail head. Shall we go?"

"Sure." Ronnie took a step to get back in the car, and then turned back to him. "Steve?"

He stopped at the front of the car hood. "Yeah, Ronnie?"

"I love you."

He stared. A smile rose up. He rushed back and grabbed her again, embracing tighter this time. "I love you, too, Ronnie."

Tears fell out of her eyes. This felt right. Natural. She belonged with this man.

~*~

How long Steve had waited, praying she would find peace about her father and learn to love him. He never gave up the hope. Now here they were, his prayers answered. Like a kid at Christmas, he'd received the second best gift of all. Without God's gift of Jesus, none of this could have happened. His faith led to her love. The elation inside bubbled up, waiting to explode out of him. He kept it at bay, reluctantly.

He pulled into the muddy parking lot of the trail head grinning like a fool. Sunshine had softened the recent snowfall. *She is so beautiful.* He couldn't take his eyes off her as she donned her winter hat and got her snowshoes out from behind her seat.

They strapped the shoes on, slipped the small backpacks on, and headed into the trees. The shadows prevented the snow from melting. The trail meandered up into the forest with a fair climb in elevation. The necessary wide gait winded them, but they kept trudging through. The path switch-backed a few times until they reached a rocky area.

Steve stopped and let her catch up to him. He took a swig of water. "Look at that view." He pointed behind them.

They had gotten high enough to be able to look over the tree tops.

The top of Mt. Evans glistened with white diamonds against the clear blue sky in the distance.

He handed her a water bottle.

"Wow," Ronnie whispered. "It never ceases to amaze me how beautiful Colorado is."

Steve reached his arm around her shoulders and they stood there in awe of their quiet, snowy surroundings. He looked toward the towering rocks ahead of them. "Bet I can beat you to the rocks."

~*~

Ronnie turned and saw that boyish gleam in his eyes. "Are you really going to try that again?"

He took off at a sprint.

Not about to miss the challenge, she slapped her lead snowshoe onto the trail to take off after him. Once again, he had gotten a good head start. She watched her footing as well as where he headed. The snow depth was deeper off to the side of the trail as evident by the tips of bushes peeking through the powder.

Steve made it to the rocks and worked his way up between two large boulders, taunting and laughing all the way.

"You cheated again," she hollered up to him.

"Aw, you just can't keep up." In a split second, he disappeared.

She stopped, stared and called out to him. "Steve?" She ran as best she could in the awkward shoes. "Steve? Where'd you go?" Making her way around the rock was difficult with the snow depth and bushes surrounding the area. She got around one of the boulders.

Steve was kneeling in the snow, waiting. In one hand he extended a red rose, the other held a small velvet box with the lid open and the most beautiful diamond ring, reflecting rainbows from the sunlight bouncing it off the surrounding rocks.

Ronnie tried to say something, anything, but no words could form on her lips.

~*~

Steve hoped the red rose didn't look too shabby after hiding under his jacket all morning. He had put it into one of those little water tubes in an attempt to keep it somewhat fresh. It was a bit flattened, but he had been able to plump it up while he hid behind the rock waiting for her. Was his assumption premature? Was she ready for this? Despite his nerves, he was determined to be ready just in case.

He swallowed hard. "Ronnie, I love you. I want to fill your life with fun surprises. I want us to experience adventures together as husband and wife. I pray you will accept. Will you marry me?"

Her face showed no sign of acceptance.

Had he blown it again? Was she not ready for a life with him?

Quick wisps of fog escaped between her lips, but her expression held...what was it? He couldn't decipher it.

Then a small tear formed in the corner of her eye and spilled over the edge, causing a rivulet to run down her cheek. Her lips curled up on each side.

"Steve..."

He gulped.

"You've rescued me off mountains and now you've rescued my heart from pain. Now that I can love God again, loving you will be easy. I would love to spend the rest of my life with you. Yes! Rescue me." She flung herself into his arms.

He slammed his fist over the box as she knocked him backwards into the snow. Her hands framed his face and she bent her head until her lips brushed his. He kissed her with the deep passion that welled up inside from being held back so long.

She kissed him back with an equal amount of love.

Shoving upward, he righted both of them, and then stood. He pulled her up, opened his fist and the box, took the ring out and placed it on her finger. He kissed her hand and fingers, and then wrapped his arms around her. He held her back just a little and looked deep into her eyes. "No, Ronnie, you've just rescued me!"

"Cast all your anxiety on Him for He cares for you."

Thank you…

for purchasing this Harbourlight title. For other
inspirational stories, please visit our on-line bookstore
at www.pelicanbookgroup.com.

For questions or more information, contact us at
customer@pelicanbookgroup.com.

Harbourlight Books
The Beacon in Christian Fiction™
an imprint of Pelican Ventures Book Group
www.pelicanbookgroup.com

Connect with Us
www.facebook.com/Pelicanbookgroup
www.twitter.com/pelicanbookgrp

To receive news and specials, subscribe to our bulletin
http://pelink.us/bulletin

May God's glory shine through
this inspirational work of fiction.

AMDG

Free Book Offer

We're looking for booklovers like you to partner with us! Join our team of influencers today and receive at least one free eBook per month. Maybe more!

For more information
Visit http://pelicanbookgroup.com/booklovers
or e-mail
booklovers@pelicanbookgroup.com